REX ZERO

AND
THE END
OF THE
WORLD

ALSO BY TIM WYNNE-JONES

STORIES

Lord of the Fries and Other Stories

The Book of Changes: Stories

Some of the Kinder Planets

NOVELS

The Uninvited

Rex Zero, King of Nothing

Rex Zero, The Great Pretender

A Thief in the House of Memory

The Boy in the Burning House

Stephen Fair

The Maestro

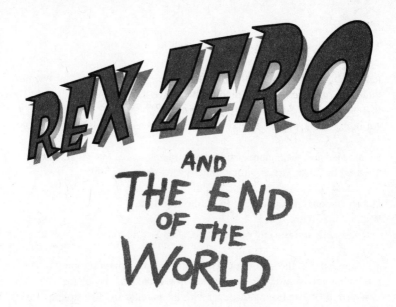

REX ZERO

AND THE END OF THE WORLD

TIM WYNNE-JONES

SQUARE
FISH

FARRAR STRAUS GIROUX • NEW YORK

SQUARE
FISH

An Imprint of Macmillan

Library of Congress Cataloging-in-Publication Data
Wynne-Jones, Tim.
     Rex Zero and the end of the world / Tim Wynne-Jones.
          p.   cm.
     Summary: In the summer of 1962 with everyone nervous about a possible nuclear war, ten-nearly-eleven-year-old Rex, having just moved to Ottawa from Vancouver with his parents and five siblings, faces his own personal challenges as he discovers new friends and a new understanding of the world around him.
     ISBN 978-0-312-64460-4
     [1. Moving, Household—Fiction.   2. Family life—Canada—Fiction. 3. Friendship—Fiction.   4. Coming of age—Fiction.   5. Cold War— Fiction.   6. Ottawa (Ont.)—History—20th century—Fiction. 7. Canada—History—1945— —Fiction.]

PZ7.W993 Rex 2007
[Fic]—dc22

                                                              2006045172

Originally published in Canada by Groundwood Books
First published in the United States by Farrar Straus Giroux
First Square Fish Edition: March 2013
Designed by Irene Metaxatos
Square Fish logo designed by Filomena Tuosto
mackids.com
10 9 8 7 6 5 4 3 2 1
LEXILE: 680L

THIS BOOK IS FOR MUM
1916–2005

REX ZERO

AND
THE END
OF THE
WORLD

THE END OF THE WORLD

I hear the bicycle before I see it. I swing around to see a boy racing down the wide gravel path through the park toward me. There's an awful squawking coming from a horn bolted onto his handlebars. He's got his finger down hard on the button and people are jumping out of his way, grabbing up toddlers, steering prams onto the grass.

Seeing him coming straight for me, I go all wobbly on my own bike and end up falling over just as he whooshes past with his head low over the handlebars and his tail up in the air. I want to yell something at him but the kid looks scared. Really scared. I get myself up, unruffle my feathers, and take a look back in the direction he came from. I don't know what I'm expecting to see. A stampede of longhorns? Killer bees? King Kong?

Then I notice the old man. The old man with the sign.

It's the summer of 1962 and there is a man in the park with a sign that says the end of the world is coming. He even knows the date—October 23. Except he has trouble with his *b*'s and *d*'s, so the sign says OCTODER. The words and numbers are printed in black ink on bright yellow bristol board stapled to a stick. In even bigger words printed in red ink the sign says, PREPARE TO MEET THY GOB.

Is that what the kid on the bike is afraid of?

The sign doesn't say how the world is going to come to an end, but the placard man looks as if he's expecting a flood. He's wearing galoshes and a mack, except I know that's not what you call them in this country. The only people around here who use words like *galoshes* and *mack* are my family. These are the kind of words you find in the *Eagle Annual*, which my grandparents send me from England every Christmas. But whatever you want to call what the placard man is wearing, it's rain gear: big black boots, a yellow raincoat as bright as his sign, and one of those clear plastic emergency rain caps that you can fold up to the size of a package of Wrigley's Juicy Fruit gum. My mother has one of those caps in her purse—or she used to. One day, when I had nothing to do—and I never have anything to do these days—I folded it up to *half* the size of a pack of gum and then, to make sure it stayed folded, I ironed it.

The clear plastic emergency cap has bands you can tie under your chin. The placard man has his tied on tight, but you can't see the bow because of his thick grizzled beard. His hair, under the clear plastic hat, looks like a nest of snakes. His skin is yellow. Not as yellow as his sign, but yellow any-

4

way, in a sort of grayish, greenish kind of way. His face is pretty grimy, too, and his eyes are sad like a basset hound's.

Who wouldn't be sad if the world was going to end?

The scared boy leaps off his bike at the west-end steps and manhandles it up to Lyon Street. Then he's gone.

I look back at the end-of-the-world man. He's dressed for rain but there isn't a cloud in the sky. And if his prediction is right, the world isn't going to end for more than three months.

In three months I'll be in a new school. If school doesn't work out—and if the old man is right—at least I won't be there for long! We just moved to Ottawa and I don't know anyone. Every day I ride down to Adams Park on my trusty steed, Diablo, named after the Cisco Kid's speedy pinto.

"Vous m'croyez fou?" shouts the end-of-the-world man, tapping his plastic-covered skull. *"Regardez autour de vous!"*

He looks as if he's asking me if I think he's crazy.

I shake my head, which is a lie, but my mother always says that a person should be polite, especially to crazy people. I shake my head again. He growls. Even his growl sounds French.

Nobody spoke French back in Vancouver. I'll have to take French when I start at my new school. Everyone in my class will be able to speak French and all I will be able to say is *Merci Bon Dieu*, which is from a song on the new Harry Belafonte album my mum got from the Capitol Record Club. I'm learning all the words from "Merci Bon Dieu" so I'll be able to talk to kids in my new class when they are speaking French.

"Get away from me!" shouts the end-of-the-world man.

He's talking to a squirrel now. In English. He must be bilingual. The squirrel skitters away. Maybe the squirrel only speaks English.

We follow the man, Diablo and I, just for something to do, but cautiously, like Harry Lime in *The Third Man* trailing his elusive quarry. I make sure I hang way back. He smells pretty ripe. A couple of lovers strolling up the path have to stop holding hands as he walks right between them. They hold their noses instead.

A little kid playing catch with his mother misses the ball and it rolls right up to the man's big black boots. He stares down at the red, white, and blue ball and growls at it, making the little kid cry and run to his mother.

She collects the ball, giving the old guy the evil eye. "Why don't you take your end of the world some place else?" she says.

The end-of-the-world man looks back at me and I shrug. Then he looks down at where the ball was and his sign droops a bit.

He glances at me again and I wave. "Leave me alone!" he shouts. *"Vous pensez que j'ignore ce que vous complotez?"*

Merci Bon Dieu.

As I watch him walk away, his clothes remind me of something. I *do* have something to do today. A new Paint by

Numbers set. It's called *Toilers of the Sea*, and the men in it are dressed like the man with the placard, except they have sou'westers on their heads, not cute little clear plastic emergency rain caps.

I spin Diablo around and head for home, pumping hard. I can already smell the oil paint.

PAINT BY NUMBERS

I used to love coloring books, but what can you do with a box of crayons? Not much. Cowboys end up with yellow Stetsons. Long John Silver ends up Long John Violet. And Dumbo? What color is Dumbo? You stare and stare at the eight colors in the box, trying to think which is closest to gray. Pink? So now you've got a pink elephant with very large ears. He's not only a freak of nature; he's a *pink* freak. So you press hard—so hard that the wax is as thick as an elephant's hide. It's the best you can do. With his problems, Dumbo is going to need a really thick skin.

Paint by Numbers has lots of colors. This one on my desk has forty-two. Forty-two! And you get *two* paintbrushes: a really thin one and one that's even thinner.

Toilers of the Sea. Three men in macks, rubber boots, and sou'westers in a sailing boat, going who knows where. The boat isn't big enough for hauling fish. I don't see any fishing gear, either. So maybe they're heading out to the island in the distance for a picnic. The sea is choppy, the sky stormy.

I flex my fingers. Those toilers have no idea what's in store for them.

I love all the little pots of paint. *Real* oil paint. Paint by Numbers is like grownup art: seascapes and sunsets and horses and mountains, just like the paintings in the National Art Gallery up on Elgin Street. My oldest sister, Cassiopeia, took me there because Mum made her. She hung around near a portrait of some famous woman while I went and looked at all the battles and tigers killing horses and Jesus or somebody with thousands of arrows in him.

The National Art Gallery is great. One day I hope one of my Paint by Numbers will hang there.

I'm ready to begin. With *Toilers of the Sea* I decide I'm going to switch the numbers around. Color number 1 will become color number 42, and so on. This is a big decision. You see, pot number 1 contains a creamy, ivory kind of color and number 42 is something dark, as if they ground up burnt trees to make it. I renumber every pot with a grease pencil: 1 becomes 42; 2 becomes 41; 3 becomes 40, et cetera.

Those toilers of the sea are in for a big surprise! I'm going to turn their world inside out. Which is kind of what it feels like for me, moving to a new place.

I live in the House of Punch. That's what I call this new place because of the huge bound collection of *Punch* magazines I found in the basement, along with a quiver full of arrows sitting on a heavy old table that looks as if it might have come from far-off Rangoon.

The owner of this house we're renting must be an explorer or something. The arrows are real Indian arrows and the quiver is made of real animal skin. You can smell the animal when you hold the quiver close to your nose.

Who shot it? What did the hunter use to kill the animal he made the quiver out of? He couldn't have used arrows unless he was just running around carrying them in his hand, which would make shooting pretty difficult.

The hide is stiff with age. The arrows clatter around inside. The feathers are ratty and laced with cobwebs.

The *Punch* magazines are old, too. They have cartoons in them, but the captions are way too long and I can never figure out what the joke is.

The House of Punch is a big house, which means we must be on our feet again. Our life is like a board game of big houses and little houses and sometimes hardly any house at all. When that happens, I feel like Eeyore in *The House at Pooh Corner* just after Pooh and Piglet accidentally move his new house. Maybe life is a board game, but I never get to roll the dice.

I pause from painting the face of one of the toilers. The colors of his face are supposed to be 37 and 39, which means that in my version they are 6 and 4: a kind of sickly yellow and an apple green. He doesn't look as if he likes sailing all that much. Or maybe he's thinking about the sandwiches they packed for their picnic.

Once, in grade three, I got the wrong lunch. I was excited because it was made with real Wonder Bread instead of homemade. Then I took a bite and it was egg and peanut butter.

I check my watch. It's time to look out the window. I try to check once an hour, at least.

Our new house is tall, and my room is in the attic, tucked between sloping walls. My desk is right in front of the window between the eaves. The window is open and tendrils of ivy peek over the sill like the skinny fingers of a burglar.

First I check for the library police. I don't know what kind of uniforms they wear, but I'm expecting them any day. When I unpacked my stuff after we moved here, I found a book from the West Vancouver Public Library. It's on my bookshelf now but with a different cover, kind of like an undercover agent. I should be okay as long as they don't bring sniffer dogs.

Next I look for anyone who appears suspicious. This is the nation's capital, after all, and there are probably Russian spies everywhere. I know what Russian army uniforms look like because I saw Russian soldiers on television on May Day, thousands of them marching past Mr. Khrushchev, the premier of the U.S.S.R. Behind the soldiers were all these missiles pulled by trucks.

In Vancouver, when we had a parade, there were floats

with Santa or Mickey Mouse on them or castles made of roses. The Russians have way better parades. But I don't expect spies would be stupid enough to walk around in uniform.

I see an old woman walking a huge dog, a nun, a gardener, and a man walking briskly with a briefcase.

Why isn't he at the office? He stops and talks to the nun.

Then I see Annie Oakley. She's hiding behind a tree. She's watching the nun and the businessman. Something is up!

I almost call out but I stop myself. I don't want to blow her cover. She's onto them—my own sister. Who knew she was so smart? She's thirteen. Usually, by thirteen people start getting dumb. Or at least girls do.

I ought to know. I've got three older sisters.

I wish I had a bow to use with those arrows from the basement, just in case Annie runs into any trouble. But after a few moments the businessman and the nun move on in separate directions. I didn't see one of them pass over a secret document. But maybe Annie did. She waits, then follows the nun toward Bank Street.

I go back to painting. The sea is turning out to be an interesting shade of pink.

Downstairs, Letitia starts to sing scales. Do re mi fa so la ti do. She's sixteen. She sings all the time. It's kind of like a disease. My father is Welsh and he says a lot of people in

Wales sing all the time, which is why he left. Too bad for him about Letitia.

There are six of us kids. There's Cassiopeia, Letitia, Annie Oakley, then me. After me, there's Flora Bella and Rupert the Sausage. He's almost four and Mum says he is the very last one. Cassie calls him her little sausage in heaven.

And here he is now. I turn around and he's walking through my door with his thumb in his mouth.

He is kind of cute but he's not supposed to come into my room without knocking. The thing is, I left the door open and I don't really mind, today.

"What is that?" he asks, putting his chin on his chubby little fists that are resting on my desktop.

"What do you think?"

He looks puzzled. "Is that blue thing a boat?" I nod but he still looks puzzled. I look at him and get an idea. I put down my tiny brush.

"I know why you're here."

"Why?"

"Because you've finally decided you want to go down the laundry chute."

His eyes grow wide with terror and he backs away. "No," he says. "I don't."

"It'll be *so* much fun," I tell him. "You'll go *so* fast." By now, I'm cleaning off my brush on an old pajama top. "We'll put six pillows at the bottom. You won't feel a thing."

The Sausage is stumbling backward toward the door. "I'm telling Mummy," he says as he leaves. He looks ready to cry.

I shrug and turn back to my desk. "Have it your own way."

I knew he wouldn't do it and it's too bad. This is the first house we've had with a laundry chute. There are openings on every floor where you can put your dirty clothes. It goes all the way down to the basement. The Sausage, Flora Bella, and I have dropped everything down that hole: dolls and soldiers and books, a bunch of carrots, and a whole bowl of popcorn.

Once we dropped one of the Sausage's teddies.

"Owww!" cried Teddy when he hit the bottom. That's what we thought, at first. Then a voice came echoing up the chute.

"Do that one more time and I'll be after you with the wooden spoon."

Mum.

Flora Bella and I had to cover our mouths to stop from howling with laughter. We imagined Mum down there in the basement piling up dirty laundry, probably humming the latest song the Capitol Records people sent her, and then— *thunk!*—Teddy lands right on her neck, like a cowboy on a bucking bronco.

I go back to my painting. Downstairs, Letitia stops singing. The Sausage is probably telling her what I said, which is better than telling Mum because Letitia will just give him a hug and he'll be okay. She's the nice sister.

Then I hear a car arrive. I look out the window. It's Dad in his new Pontiac. We used to be Ford people, but now we're Pontiac people. Does that mean we've gone up or down in the world?

I hear doors shutting and feet galumphing downstairs as too many sisters and one little brother go to greet Dad home from work. I just keep painting, not because I don't want to see Dad but because I've got about half of the painting done and I want to see how it turns out. If you use the right numbers, then you already know it's going to turn out just like the picture on the front. Not mine.

Suddenly there is a knock at the open door.

It's Dad.

"May I come in, chum?" he asks. What's he doing coming all the way up to the attic?

I nod and he strides over to my desk. He's wearing a three-piece tweed suit and his Royal Engineers' tie with the red and blue stripes. His pipe is in his mouth. He scruffles my hair, leans on the back of my chair, and looks over my shoulder at the painting.

"Bad day at sea?" he asks. He tamps down the tobacco in his pipe with this great little silver gizmo. I watch him, waiting. Finally he gets his pipe drawing just right.

"Do you know what day it is?" he says.

In summer it's hard to know. Wednesday? But is that

what he means? Is it my mother's birthday? There are eight people in the family; the only birthday I ever remember for sure is my own, which is not until August 12.

"Well?"

"Wednesday?"

"And what happens on Wednesdays?"

Garbage? Taking the dog for a walk?

I look at him and he's got this glint in his eye.

"The stock-car races!" He nods. "Hadn't you better round up some bottle caps?" He glances at his watch. "You should have just enough time before dinner. Chop-chop."

I race downstairs and out to the street. I need six Pure Spring bottle caps to get in free at Lansdowne Park as long as Dad pays full fare. I can get them at the Clemow Smoke Shop. The owner, Mr. Papazian, lets me raid the little container under the bottle opener that's attached to the big freezer.

As I open the door, another boy comes rushing out and heads up Bank Street in a big hurry. I think maybe he shoplifted something but Mr. Papazian is smiling behind the counter.

"Rex," he says. "Here for more bottle caps?" I nod and look back up Bank Street. The boy stops and looks back. I wave but he isn't looking at me. There's a van pulled up to the curb and a man rolling a big box into it. The van is full of boxes big enough for a washing machine or a stove.

I close the door and head inside.

"Have you made a friendship yet?" asks Mr. Papazian, giving me change for two cents' worth of licorice.

I shake my head.

"My boys," he says. "Same thing. They had trouble when we moved here, too."

"What happened to them?"

He shrugs and closes the till. "They are gone now."

Just what I was afraid of. I thank him for the bottle caps and the licorice and head out the door.

What happened to all the boys my age?

The only ones I see are always in a hurry. I know that there are two kinds of hurries: hurrying to something and hurrying away from something. All I see are boys hurrying away. Where is everyone going?

A GROWL IN THE NIGHT

I had a white car once, a long time ago. It was a kiddy-car convertible with pedals. There's a picture of me sitting in it with baby Flora Bella on my lap. The picture was taken in England, where we lived until I was almost four. It's easy to tell it was England because I'm wearing a tie. My mother made me wear a tie and flannel shorts and kneesocks even when we moved to Canada.

A tie is a lot of extra work. A kid wants you to go out and play and you have to say, "All right. Just let me put on my tie."

That getup attracted bullies like an old cup of chocolate attracts mold. I got beaten up because of the way I dressed. Well, what really happened was I said *garage* as if it rhymed with *carriage* and I guess the bully didn't like the way it sounded. So my accent was the problem, but I don't think the tie helped.

But I was talking about my little white car.

The memory of it comes back to me because there is a big white car parked on Clemow Avenue when I get back from the stock-car races and have to take Kincho for a walk. I'm too wired up to sleep, my mother says, but I don't want to take Kincho out.

"It's too dark," I say.

"The moon is almost full," says my father.

"What about strangers?"

"Kincho will take care of any strangers."

"Have you noticed how few kids there are around here?" I say. "I think something's happening to them."

They both laugh.

"Off you go, son. Chop-chop."

"But think about Little Billy Turvey," I say, desperately. "Look what happened to him." It was in all the papers.

"The poor lad drowned," says my mother. "We're not asking you to get yourself drowned."

"But the police think he may have been picked up by a stranger first, and the stranger drowned him!"

They both laugh, again. Then my father scruffles my hair and says that if I do get picked up by a stranger, he'll let me go soon enough because I talk too much.

"Besides," he says, "Little Billy Turvey was five. You're a great big strapping lad of ten."

"Almost eleven."

"There," says my mother. "You see?"

I *don't* see. I want to let them know that Little Billy

Turvey's own father said, in the papers, that Billy was very trusting and liked people and if anyone offered him a nickel to go for a ride in a car, he would have taken it. I want to remind them that *I* am very trusting and *I* like people and *I* might accidentally do the same thing even though I'm twice Billy's age.

But before I know it, Dad has Kincho cinched up to his choke chain and me cinched up to Kincho's wide black leash and he's dragging me down the front steps—Kincho, not my dad. Out into the street and out into the dark. I hold on with both hands like a water-skier behind some crazy, furry black motorboat.

"Stay away from the canal," my father calls after me, and bursts out laughing. Parents can be so cruel.

Kincho is a perfect example. The Sausage started having this terrible dream just after we moved here about a black monster named Kincho, who had long, sharp teeth and was always trying to eat him. So what did my parents do? They went to the Humane Society and found a stray dog just like the monster in the dream and brought him home. He is a cross between a Labrador retriever and a Sherman tank. And I have to walk him because my older sisters always get out of it. It's not fair. My arms already ache before we get halfway down the block.

And then I see the beautiful white car.

There is no one in it, which is lucky because Kincho

pees on the rear tire right away and then heads for the front one. He can't stop sniffing that car.

I've never seen anything like it before. It says Citroën on the front and it looks like a car from the future. It's so low to the ground and streamlined and so white.

A spy's car. A good spy. I don't know what happened to my little white kiddy car. Just another of the things that got lost when we moved here. Somebody rolls the dice and you move to a space that says, "Lose one white car." What can you do? But I bet a Citroën is what my car would have wanted to be when it grew up.

I hear someone opening a door in a house nearby and I drag Kincho away in a hurry. Laughter spills out of the house as I slip into the shadows behind a tall hedge. Soon the laughter dies and all I can hear are the cicadas and manly footsteps and a car door open and shut. I step out of the shadows to watch the Citroën glide soundlessly by.

I turn down Lyon Street toward the park. It's nice out. It's not scary at all. Not with Kincho. But even though I'm not really scared, I start thinking about Little Billy Turvey again. I can't help it.

Just a week ago, I was leaning on the railing down near the Pretoria Bridge, watching the police dragging the canal. It was like *Sea Hunt*, only it was the Rideau Canal instead of the ocean. I peered down into the murky depths, expecting to see a body floating up to the surface. Little Billy had been going to a movie with his sister, who was about my age, when suddenly he wasn't with his sister anymore. What happened? What if I took the Sausage to a movie and lost him?

Kincho stops at the top of the steps that lead down into Adams Park. He sits, which is kind of amazing. I didn't know he knew how. It gives us both a chance to catch our breath.

I look at the park stretching out before me. The moon is low in the sky, so all the shadows seem to be pointing right at me. I've never been out this late alone, and it's kind of exciting. The park is long and sinewy, like a snake. The paths look white under the moon. It's so quiet. Dead quiet, dark and empty. It smells of nothing but cool greenness. I sit down on the top step beside the dog, with my arm around his neck. If Adams Park were a stadium like Lansdowne Park, these would be the dollar bleachers.

Then I hear something—I'm not sure what—but Kincho hears it, too, and both our heads swivel toward the wall of trees flanking the north side of the park. I don't see anything moving—anything except the trees. If Kincho sees anything, he isn't saying, but he's on red alert, I can tell. The breeze picks up and the trees seem to turn their heads to look up the field, like fans watching a car spin out of control on the northeast turn. We follow their gaze, Kincho and me. He growls low in his throat.

"What is it, boy?"

He growls again and suddenly takes off down the steps. I

let go of his leash just in time so that I don't get dragged down the steps face-first.

"Kincho!"

I race after him, down into the dark, but he's way ahead of me. He veers off the path and out of the lamplight. I can hardly see him against the swaying blackness of the trees.

Then I almost fall over him because he stops suddenly. He growls again and the hackles on his neck rise. Picking up his leash I wrap it tightly around my fist several times and kneel beside him, trying to get my breath back and hold him still. I can feel his doggy engines rumbling. The grass is heavy with dew, which soaks through the knees of my jeans.

"Shhhhh, fella. What is it?" I follow his gaze. A tiny light flashes about forty or fifty yards away, right near the underbrush. I watch and wait.

It happens again, a little farther along.

A firefly, I think. But Kincho doesn't think so. His engines are really rumbling now.

I stand up very slowly. Holding his leash tightly, I move toward the wall of trees. I can see someone, backlit by the lights from Bank Street. A person squatting right in the spot where I saw the flash of light. There is another tiny flash and I realize what he's doing. He's taking pictures.

Flash.

I edge closer until I'm only about thirty yards away.

It's a kid. Kincho is straining to get away but the photographer doesn't seem to notice.

Then I hear a rustling in the bush and stop dead in my tracks. The rustling is too noisy to be a squirrel. Too noisy to be the wind.

Kincho starts to growl again and I let out a little moan—I can't help it.

Then all at once there is a huge growling noise from the bushes, a high-pitched scream, and a terrible loud bark from Kincho.

The photographer backs up so quickly he falls over. He jumps to his feet and takes off. Kincho starts barking like crazy and dragging me closer and closer toward that huge growling thing in the undergrowth. The growling doesn't sound anything like a dog. I plant my feet and pull backward for all I'm worth, until Kincho is up on his back feet, gasping and wheezing from the choke chain tightening around his neck. Still he barks this raspy bark and I hold on like the last guy in a tug-of-war. Meanwhile, the photographer is running toward Bank Street, and there is something really weird about the way he runs but I don't have time to figure out what because the creature in the bushes growls again, nearer to me.

Then I see it.

Just for one terrible second. A shadow low to the ground emerges from the undergrowth. A dark rounded shoulder and a hunched black head. It tilts back its head and roars.

And then it is gone again, crashing back into the woods.

Kincho whines, then barks and growls and dances and

spins around, trying to get free, trying to follow it. He yips and prances and wraps me up in his leash until I fall over.

"You crazy dog. Stop it!" I scramble to my feet again and start heading back toward the Lyon Street exit. "Come on!" I hiss. *"Come on!"*

I'm running now and the dog runs, too, but then he changes his mind and almost yanks my shoulder off.

"Owwww!"

I look back. The photographer has made it to the east end of the park and races up the steps to Bank Street. He turns and the streetlight is right above him now, which is when I realize what was weird about the way he was running.

It's not a him, it's a her! A girl with shoulder-length hair. The light is golden on her head, like a crown or a halo. She stops only for a fraction of a second before she takes off, but the image is burned into my brain, as if I were the camera.

MUTANTS AND SPIES

I sit on the edge of my bed in my pajamas spinning the chamber of my six-gun, loading bullets one by one. The revolver is silver with real-pearl-looking handle grips. I know I'm too old for toy guns, but back in West Vancouver, my friends and I were the marshals of the woods along the mountain. A desperado didn't stand a chance.

I close the chamber and give it a final twirl. This gun is so good my friends all agreed that when one of them got shot, they had to stay dead until they counted seventy-five steamboats instead of just fifty. I can see them lying all over the hillside back home, still counting.

There's a noise at my door and I look up. It's Annie Oakley. She's in her pajamas, too. They have lariats all over them and cactuses and rattlers. She has the best pajamas. Mine are blue with planets: Saturns and Jupiters and Marses—big deal.

She's leaning on my door frame with her arms folded on her chest. She's frowning at me. When I look into her eyes under the fringe of curly brown hair, I know she's come snooping.

"What happened?" she says.

I fire off a round at a sock lying helplessly on the floor. *Bang!*

"There was this thing in the park." I glance at her. She's still listening. I look for the other sock—probably hiding behind the box of books I haven't put on the shelf yet. "And there was this girl taking pictures—but she ran away."

Annie looks at my gun.

"I'm not making it up," I say.

To my surprise, she nods and her frown gets angrier, but I can tell she isn't angry at me. "Everything is all wrong," she says. Then she strides over to my desk. The lamp is still on and she stares at my painting for a bit. "This is the ugliest one yet."

"Thanks."

She straddles the chair, back to front, and folds her arms along the backrest like a gunslinger. She rests her chin on her arms.

"This thing," she said. "Did you see it?"

"Just for a second. Just part of it."

"Was it a monster?"

I hesitate, not sure if she's making fun of me. "I don't know what it was. It sure growled a lot."

"Probably a mutant," she says. "It's because of the fallout. In Hiroshima, a woman gave birth to a baby with two heads but only three eyes. Another woman gave birth to a giant squid. That's what radiation does."

I know about Hiroshima. That's where the Americans dropped the first atomic bomb. But I didn't know about people giving birth to giant squids.

I shudder.

"It's not just in Japan either," says Annie, and her eyes get all fiery. "There are cases in the States of people who live too close to nuclear-weapons test zones and who turn into raving, homicidal mutants."

I laugh before I can stop myself.

"What are you laughing at?" Annie narrows her eyes. "You are such a numbskull." Her fists are curled and I don't want to fight. She hardly ever talks to me and I don't want her to go, especially not now.

"Sorry," I say quickly.

Suddenly I remember seeing her from my window earlier that afternoon. I was so excited about going out with Dad, I forgot to ask her about it.

"You were spying," I say. She directs her glare my way and I want to duck and cover. "The nun and the businessman. I saw you."

I can see the wheels turning. She's trying to decide whether to tell me or not. I try to look extra smart and brave and trustworthy. "That nun," I say, lowering my voice, "she looked pretty suspicious to me."

Annie's eyes light up. "You're right," she whispers. "For one thing, nuns are usually women."

I gasp. It's true. Why didn't I think about that? The nun didn't look anything like a woman.

"It would be a perfect disguise," I say. "Everybody trusts nuns."

She nods gravely. "I've been following *her* for weeks. She has some pretty strange friends."

"What did they say?"

Annie stands up and swings the chair around so that she can sit in it properly and then she leans forward, lowering her voice. "The *businessman* asked her if *Father* was back from his *visit* in the *East*."

I nod, waiting. She doesn't say anything, but there is an expectant gleam in her eyes.

"Code?"

She nods. "Who do you think *Father* is? What kind of a *visit* do you think he's on? Where in the *East* do you think he got to?

I shake my head; the possibilities are endless. "What did the nun say?"

Now Annie's eyes are blazing. "She—if she really is a she—said, '*I expect he'll have good news for us.*' "

I pull my legs up to my chest. She's right. That's more than a little suspicious.

Annie pulls her chair closer to the bed. "There was this

guy," she whispers. "It was in the papers. He went underground to see how much Communist activity there was in Ottawa. He said there are twenty-four Communist Party members in the city."

It doesn't sound like much. I'm kind of disappointed and it must show on my face because Annie's eyebrows go up and up until they disappear under her fringe of curls.

"That can't be right," I finally say.

She smiles mysteriously. "You've got it, brother," she says. "Believe me. There are way more than that. I'm keeping a list."

She gets up and leans over my desk to look out the window, as if maybe some of those Communists might be right outside. The window is open and a breeze blows her hair a bit. Her hair is always a snarled mess. Mum can never catch her to comb it.

Annie is scanning the street. But all I can think about is that she said I was right about something. She's never said that before. Even better, she called me "brother." I've always wondered whether we could really be related. She's so brave—not afraid of anything.

"Have you made any friends yet?" I ask.

She doesn't turn, just shrugs.

"Friends are overrated," she says, never taking her eyes off the street below.

"Oh," I say.

She sniffs and crosses her arms again. "If you don't have any friends, no one can ever betray you."

It's a good point, I guess. "I haven't," I say. "Made any friends, I mean." I try to make it sound like it's no big deal. "The weird thing is that there's hardly anyone my age around. Have you noticed that?" She looks at me, interested again. "Whenever I see anyone my age they're always running away like something is after them."

She looks back out the window. "Maybe they're being snatched."

I remember the van on Bank Street with all those big boxes in the back. What was really in those boxes?

"They're probably doing tests on them," I say. "Radiation tests."

She nods. "Everything is all wrong," she says again.

She leaves without another word. I climb under the covers and turn off my bedside light. I don't know why, but it doesn't seem so bad to be alone anymore. I rest my head on my arm. I feel a little better. But I've got my six-gun under my pillow, just in case.

RINGING BELLS

have a dream that night. There are these men picking up kids and taking them away in vans. "You'll be a lot safer where we're taking you," this woman says. She's ticking off a name on a list as a kid walks up the plank into the van. "What about me, ma'am?" I ask. But no one even notices I'm there.

The next morning me and Diablo go back to Adams Park. I don't find any mauled bodies or mutant footprints, but I do find a flashbulb over by the bushes.

So there was a photographer. I watch the people in the park pushing prams—no, buggies. It looks so safe that I get up the courage to poke my head into the bushes and have a look around.

There is nothing here. It's kind of nice. The leaves are wet and cool against my bare arms and legs. A tiny bird twitters. A frog leaps. A garter snake slithers by.

I'm almost disappointed. I move in a little deeper and

the warmth of the sunlight slides off my back. The greenness closes in around me.

The underbrush is thick. That thing—the mutant—could be hiding anywhere.

I listen. I don't hear anything unusual at first. Then I think I hear a bell. It sounds like the handbell the knife sharpener uses when he walks up the street pushing his grindstone on its little wheels.

Some thorny stem scratches my leg. I look down. I'm bleeding a little but it's nothing. I lick my finger and rub away the blood.

That's when I notice something caught on the same thorns but higher up.

A hank of thick shiny black hair.

I touch it. It's soft. I gather it into a ball, a whole handful of it. I hold it up to my nose. It smells musty. It could have come from anything. A squirrel, maybe. A pretty big squirrel.

There are still a few strands of the hair or fur or whatever it is hanging from the thorn. It's at the same height as my chest. So it would have to have been a really *tall* squirrel.

I listen again, a bit frightened now. It could be a really tall dog. I remember the shadow that emerged from the bushes last night, the thick rounded shoulder, and the thick black head.

That was no dog.

I hear another bell. There are two of them now. They seem to be coming from the park. Maybe it's the ice cream truck, I think, but the ice cream truck doesn't drive into the park.

I can't help thinking the bells are a warning. It's crazy but I start backing out of the bush anyway, clutching the fur in one hand and the flashbulb in the other. I move slowly at first. It's downhill. I slip at one point and reach out to a tree trunk for support. Suddenly the underbrush feels alive. I turn and break for the open. I burst out into the sunshine dragging bits of ivy and who knows what behind me, then I fall in a heap on the grass, breathing hard, as if I'm Lloyd Bridges on *Sea Hunt* and I've just come up from the deep.

After a moment, when I've got my breath back, I look at the bushes. Nothing.

"Hey!"

I turn around. There's a dark-haired boy straddling the bar of his bike about twenty feet away on the path.

"You shouldn't go in there," he says. His skin is dark. His eyes are dark, too, and full of concern.

I get up, pulling ivy off me.

"Why not?"

He hoists his backside onto the seat and puts his foot on the pedal. "Just stay away, okay?" he calls to me. "If you know what's good for you." Then he shoves off and rides away.

I'm so stunned it takes me a moment to get up and run for Diablo. But by the time I've put the hank of black fur in one pocket and the flashbulb in the other and wrestled my bike up off the ground, the dark boy is gone. I stand tall on the pedals but I can't see him anywhere.

I take a deep breath and head off through the park in the same direction the boy was going.

I don't find him. I don't find anyone. Where is everyone? I remember my dream and shudder. *What about me, ma'am?*

That evening I hear Cassiopeia complaining about walking the dog because she has to paint her nails and I offer to take him. I'm halfway down the block when Annie Oakley catches up with me.

"Rex," she says, "wait."

I'm glad she's here. I tell her about the boy and his warning as we walk over to the park.

We stand on the top steps at the Lyon Street entrance for about fourteen million hours taking turns holding Kincho. We don't see or hear anything mutant.

We give up and start for home. "There hasn't been anything in the papers," she says. "It's obviously a cover-up."

"What are they covering up?" I ask.

She glares at me. "The truth," she says.

Back home Mum and Dad and Cassiopeia are watching a special on CBOT called *The Titans*. It's about the rise to supremacy of the two world powers, Russia—except it's really called the Soviet Union—and the United States. Part One is about the Soviet Union.

Mum and Cassiopeia both have their hair up in curlers.

Mum is wearing a blue muumuu. Cassiopeia is all dolled up in a plaid outfit and jewelry and looks as if the queen might be dropping by later on.

Annie Oakley plunks herself down in the one remaining easy chair. I sit on the couch very quietly between Mum and Dad, waiting for one of them to notice I'm there and send me to bed. Nobody does. Mum even hands me the bowl of popcorn without noticing that it's me she's handing it to. I munch extra quietly and pass it on to Dad.

The show is scary. There are lots of pictures of dead people lying in puddles and bombs going off. It's jerky old footage but I know things are not good right now. There are riots in Berlin about the Wall. It's in the paper every day. People don't want the Wall. I can understand why. It would be terrible to have a wall right through the middle of your city.

I try to imagine a wall down the middle of Clemow Avenue. I wouldn't be able to get to Lansdowne Park, so no more stock-car races. The Rough Riders football season starts there on August 10, two days before my birthday, but I wouldn't be able to go. Mum couldn't even get to the IGA to do her shopping.

That's what it's like when they build a wall.

The TV show says that the Cold War is heating up. I'm not exactly sure what that means except that handsome President Kennedy makes threats against the Soviet Union, and Premier Khrushchev, who looks like a bald bear with squinty eyes and bad teeth, hits his desk at the UN with his shoe and makes threats against the U.S.A. The threats sound a lot worse in Russian. Sometimes there are pictures of Khrushchev smiling with his friend Fidel Castro, who has a big beard and smokes cigars and reminds me of Groucho Marx. He's the boss of Cuba and the Americans really don't like Cuba, which is too bad for them because it's right next door.

Things are not looking good.

Meanwhile, on the TV, there is a scene from World War II at Stalingrad. If I've got it right, the Russians were the good guys at Stalingrad. They defeated Hitler's Sixth Army.

Sheesh! Six armies? No wonder Hitler lost the war if he was going through armies like that! There is really good footage of the Russian Red Army cavalry on Siberian ponies just pounding the heck out of the Germans because their Panzer tanks are all frozen up. I know about Panzers. They're what General Rommel used in the desert. But it looks like they don't work so well in the snow.

The Russian soldiers wear their hats rolled down right over their faces, with holes for their eyes, nose, and mouth.

"Balaclavas," says Dad. "You need a face hat when it's that cold." He's talking to Mum right over my head. "Trust the Reds to come up with the perfect headgear for hoodlums and robbers."

They have a little laugh. They still haven't noticed me. I should try this more often.

Cassiopeia suddenly gasps and looks at her fingers. Her nails are shiny red.

"What if people think I'm a Communist sympathizer?" she says.

Dad relights his pipe. "Why don't you paint little Union Jacks on them?"

Cassiopeia stares at her fingernails for a long time, her forehead creased, as if she has to make a life-or-death decision. "I'm going to go with clear," she says finally, and unscrews the top of her nail polish remover.

"Good idea," says Mum. "Is the interview tomorrow?"

Cassie nods. "Birks Jewelers," she says. "I just can't take the chance."

Annie Oakley grinds her teeth.

"Please don't do that, dear," says Mum. "It sounds common."

Annie slams her journal shut. It's got a great skull and crossbones drawn in white on the cover.

"You think *I'm* common," says Annie. "Wait until the mutants come!" Then she leaves the room in a huff.

At ten-thirty, Letitia arrives all dressed up to watch *Peter Gunn*. Letitia's glasses have wings with rhinestones in them. Her hairband has hearts on it. She's in love with the detective Peter Gunn.

"Sorry, sweetheart," says Dad. "We're not changing the channel tonight." He wants to watch the rest of *The Titans*. Letitia leaves in a huff, too. Then Cassiopeia sighs and leaves, saying she needs her beauty sleep, which is really true.

So now it's just me and Mum and Dad on the couch in

the darkened TV room on the second floor of the House of Punch on Clemow Avenue, which doesn't have a wall down the middle of it. Yet! The commentator begins to talk about Joseph Stalin and his reign of terror. He was the Soviet leader before Khrushchev. Stalin executed lots of people. Not just his enemies, but ordinary people he didn't like.

Finally, I can't stand it anymore.

"What am I doing here?" I yell. Mum and Dad look at me with surprise. "Somebody, *please* make me go to bed!"

MOVIE STAR FRIENDS

It's a well-known fact that families move in the summer so that their children can wander around a new neighborhood for two months in lonely despair. You walk around the school you are going to attend in the fall wondering which window will be your new classroom and what your teacher will be like. Vulture, rhinoceros, wildcat, cow?

I patrol the chain-link fence of the schoolyard and check out the likely places I might get cornered by bullies. I don't wear funny clothes anymore and I know that *garage* rhymes with *mirage*. But I just hope that's enough.

I look at the curved archway of the entrance to the school. It's called Mutchmor. Mutchmor Public School. Like *much more* but spelled wrong and mashed together.

The school is really old. Maybe that's how people spelled in those days. Or maybe it's French. *Merci Bon Dieu.*

I've never biked past Mutchmor. It's at the corner of Lyon and Fifth, where Lyon Street ends. Fifth looks pretty run-down. Diablo is always a bit nervous when we get there. But today is a lemon-pie day, complete with meringue clouds, so we decide to take the plunge. And that's when we find the pollywog pond.

The pond is off a shady backstreet down by the Rideau Canal way south of my place. And what do you know? There are kids all over this neighborhood! I pass two boys playing catch. I see a girl skipping and another couple of girls my age with hula hoops. They look at me as I go by. I wave and one of them waves back, which makes her hula hoop fall off.

Nobody is running away. A good sign.

When I see the pollywog pond, I race home to get a jar. When I get back, two boys are there. They have jars, too. I find my own stretch of weedy shoreline halfway around the pond. We catch about a million pollywogs between us. I hold my jar up to the light and look through the cloudy water and darting black bodies at the two boys. They are looking through their jars at me.

"Sure are a lot of pollywogs," I say. They lower their jars and stare at me as if I'm wearing a tie.

The one with the red hair says, "They're called tadpoles."

Then the one with the dark brown hair says, "But polly-wogs is a good name."

The redhead stares at his friend. "Why?"

The dark-haired boy shrugs and looks at his bottle. "Be-cause they're so woggly."

"Oh," says the redhead.

Then they go back to talking to each other. I feel as if a disaster has been narrowly averted. I pretend to turn my attention to the teeming pond, except that I'm actually moving closer and closer so that I can hear what they're saying. Eavesdropping is a talent you develop when you move all the time. I hear one of them say the word *Mutchmor*.

"What grade?" I ask boldly.

"Six."

"Me, too. Is it an okay school?"

They look at each other and then back at me and shrug. How would they know? They've probably always gone there and have nothing to compare it to.

The redhead has a flattop. The other boy's hair is the color of Cadbury Caramilk, but he has a gray splotch the size of a quarter. I guess I must have been staring at the gray splotch because he starts to tug at it self-consciously.

"You probably won't believe this," he says, "but I'm actually seventy-six years old."

Then the other boy says, "James repeated grade four sixty times."

"Holy moly," I say. They look at each other as if maybe they think I really fell for that. "I'm not very good at school either," I say quickly. "In fact, my parents don't think I'll be able to handle Mutchmor. They're trying to get me into Much Less."

This is the kind of statement that can get you beaten up,

but these two guys don't look the type. They are boys with bikes and jars full of pollywogs or tadpoles, just like me.

After a private conference, the one named James steps forward.

"Are you really stupid?"

I make a sad expression and nod. "Ask me anything."

"What's the capital of Russia?"

"Everybody knows that. The capital of Russia is Mayberry."

A light comes on in James's eye. He turns to the redhead, who steps forward. "What color is blue?"

"Brown?"

And then he fires another one at me. "What do you get if you mix salt, ink, Ipana toothpaste, tadpoles, and instant mashed potatoes together?"

"Cheez Whiz?"

"Holy mackerel!" says James. "How'd you get to be so dumb?"

They're smiling now and step forward to introduce themselves properly.

"I'm James Stewart," says the seventy-six-year-old. "Like in *The Naked Spur*."

"And I'm Buster Keaton," says the redhead. "Like in *The General*."

So I tell them my name. "Rex Harrison," I say. "As in *The Ghost and Mrs. Muir*." They look stunned and then I hit myself in the forehead as if I forgot my own name. "I mean, Rex Norton-Norton."

"Rex Norton," says Buster. "That's a good hero's name."

"Except it's Rex Norton-Norton."

"Norton, Norton?" says Buster.

I shrug. "I know. It's kind of strange. My dad says that where he came from, Wales, there were so many Nortons they had to do something to tell them apart. So there were the plain Nortons and the Norton-Thortons and Norton-Whartons and Norton-Gortons."

"What about Norton-Snorton?" asks James.

I nod. Then I explain to them about the hyphen in my name.

"Oh, right," says Buster. "Like a minus sign." Then his eyes get big. "So really you're just plain Rex. Because your last name is Norton minus Norton which equals zero."

"I like it!" I say. "Hey, maybe I could be Rex Zero."

Buster looks pleased. "Rex Zero it is." Then he admits that his name is really Kevin Keaton but everyone always calls him Buster. But James Stewart really *is* James Stewart.

Next we go look over our bikes. We kind of sniff around them like Kincho sniffs around cars. Buster has a red Schwinn almost the same color as his flattop, and James has a gold Motobécane he picked up in France.

"His father's a Big Cheese in the government," Buster tells me. James looks uncomfortable. And who wouldn't be—having a dad who was a big cheese.

"If you're seventy-six, your dad must be really *really* old," I say. They laugh and I feel like I just scored a touchdown.

Then we admire my Raleigh. It's a green three-speed. I don't tell them it's called Diablo. I've put red and white streamers on the handle grips, but it's the speedometer that really impresses them.

"We should go out to the Hog's Back," says James. "You could get up to fifty or sixty miles per hour there, no problem."

I try to imagine what the Hog's Back is but I don't ask.

I open up my carrier bag and take out the bicycle repair kit. Buster holds up one of the weird-shaped wrenches.

"You never told us you were a spy."

"Keep it down."

Buster gives the wrench back to me. "Sure thing," he says. "But we're going to have to kill you."

Then we sprawl on the grass beside the pond and talk about spies and movies we've seen and Most Wanted criminals. I think about telling them what happened in the park and about the dark-haired boy who told me not to go into the woods, but it seems like it happened a million years ago and a million miles from here. Besides, would they believe me?

James heard that morning at breakfast that there's some guy in the States who wants Canada and America to unite because he thinks the West is losing the Cold War and we'd be a lot stronger if the whole continent were one huge country. "The United States of Canada."

We all agree that that sounds nifty.

"This guy wants the capital to be in Sioux Falls, South Dakota, which is sort of in the middle. It's also where he lives."

"Hey, it would be cool to be part of America," says Buster. "Because then we'd be a lot closer to Hollywood."

James smiles at me and looks at his watch. It's the good kind with a stretchy gold band.

"I've got to go," he says. So we all get up and guide our trusty bikes one-handed, with our jars of pollywogs cradled in the other arm. When we get to Lyon Street we ride down the middle like we own it. The lions of Lyon Street.

And here's the most amazing thing: we all live on Clemow.

"How come I've never seen you?"

"I was away at my cottage," says James.

"I was away at camp," says Buster.

"Well, that explains it," I say. We've reached the corner of Clemow and Lyon and stopped because James has to go up toward Percy, and Buster and I have to turn down toward Bank. "There were just no kids around here. It was kind of eerie. Like *The Twilight Zone*."

Buster swallows hard and his Adam's apple bobs up and down. He glances nervously at James.

"What?" I ask.

James screws up his eyes. Then he looks around. "It is *The Twilight Zone*," he says.

I stare at him. He doesn't look like he's fooling. "Really?"

He nods. "From here over to Isabella and from Percy all the way to O'Connor. You won't find many kids hanging around."

"Why?"

Buster starts to say something but James interrupts him. "Maybe we should . . . you know . . . check with . . . you know." He looks at me. "We have to talk to someone before we can tell you," he says. "What are you doing tomorrow?"

What am I doing tomorrow? I can't remember the last time someone said that to me. If I was a little let down that they wouldn't tell me the big secret, this wonderful question wipes my disappointment clear away.

"Nothing much," I say. We agree to meet at Buster's in the morning. Then I wave goodbye and wobble off.

"Rex?" James calls. I almost crash but pull myself over to the curb, spilling hardly any tadpole water. I turn to look. "Go straight home," he says.

I smile, as if he's joking. But I can tell from the James Stewart look on his face that he's dead serious.

DUMP ORBIT

T hat night I dream of Most Wanted criminals—a whole park full of them walking arm in arm with one another or playing catch or pushing buggies with tiny Most Wanted criminals in them dressed up as babies. I wake with a start and wonder why they're called Most Wanted when really nobody wants them around one bit.

My right arm is fast asleep. I hate that. You can pick up your arm and drop it on the bed like a salami. You can slug yourself in the face with your own fist! Then come the pins and needles as the blood rushes back into your arm. It hurts, but at least it means you're not dead.

I lie with my head cupped in my good hand while my right arm buzzes back to life. It's still dark. I go to the window. The pavement is washed with soft dawn colors: numbers 28, 12, and 17.

I open my window and poke my head outside. Everything smells like perfume. Shalimar, which is what Cassiopeia wears. I spilled a bottle of her Shalimar once and everything smelled like Shalimar for weeks. Everything except Cassiopeia.

I look up and down the street. No Most Wanted criminals. No mutants or spies. No library police. No Wall. The thing in the park . . . it was more than a week ago and I'd even begun to think that maybe I'd imagined it. But what James and Buster said about *The Twilight Zone* has got me wondering.

If I hang way out the window, I can almost see Buster's place. James's house is two blocks away. It will be hours before I meet up with them. I go back to bed, hoping they don't turn out to be a dream.

◎ ◎ ◎

Mum won't let me go anywhere until nine o'clock.

"They're friends, Mum. Friends don't start at nine like school!" But she doesn't care. She wants me to do something about the jar of pollywogs I left on the back stoop.

"They're called tadpoles," I explain.

"They're called filthy and revolting," says Mum.

What am I supposed to do? Turn them into frogs? Anyway, I can't go out back. Kincho is tearing up a lawn chair. He's in one of his moods. He really is like a nightmare. One minute he's okay and the next minute he's running around in circles as if he's trapped in his own personal tornado. I wish he were more like Rin Tin Tin or Lassie. Like smart, for instance.

When I finally get to Buster's house, he's not in. His mother has taken him shopping for clothes. He won't be back until late. A maid tells me this. At least I think she's a maid. She's wearing a pink uniform with white trim. At first I think she's a nurse, except that she has a feather duster under her arm.

I've never known anyone with a maid. I look past her into the house wondering how many laundry chutes they have.

James isn't in, either. No one comes to the door to tell me. No one is at home. I keep knocking anyway, just in case.

After about ten hours, I step back from the front door to look up at the windows. I half expect to see James's face disappear behind a curtain. I stand there imagining him thinking about the day before and wishing he hadn't wasted so much time with such a weird new boy. I can just see him hiding up there trying to think of ways to avoid me and my stupid jokes. He seemed to like me, but, then, he looked like one of those really nice people who likes everybody.

I look back down the street. Maybe he's with Buster. Maybe shopping with someone's mother is better than hanging around with Rex Zero. I feel the front of my shirt to make sure I'm not wearing a tie.

Eventually, I head home for lunch and then slip out again before Mum can make me look after the Sausage.

I check at Buster's and the same maid tells me to come back tomorrow. There's still no one at James's place. This is the shortest friendship I've ever had!

I head down to Adams Park, even if it is in the very middle of the twilight zone.

Today, Adams Park is a thing of beauty. The grass is so green it looks as if it's breathing. The flowers are like those choirs of flowers in *Alice in Wonderland*, singing little yellow, red, and purple songs. There's a fountain sparkling and, a long way away, an arched tunnel so you can stroll under Bank Street to another park. I wonder if it's called Eve's Park. There are benches along the winding gravel paths. It doesn't look like the twilight zone.

"Profitez du soleil tant que vous pourrez!"

It's the placard man. His sign is the same. No update on the end of the world. It's still going to happen in "Octoder." But he's wearing different clothes. He's wearing a white suit and a Hawaiian shirt but no shoes or socks. His feet look like old roots.

The suit isn't really white but it used to be. It looks as if he slept in it. It's rumpled and very, very dirty. I follow him a bit, watch him snarl at anyone who gets too close.

"Enjoy the sun while you can!" he shouts. But nobody is listening.

He stops at a drinking fountain. The real fountain stands in the middle of a pond full of lily pads. It's a statue of a fat angel shooting water out of his mouth in an excellent arc in the air. That is the kind of activity Mum will not tolerate. Flora Bella and I try it all the time.

The placard man drinks and drinks. He drinks so much I glance over at the fat angel in the pond, half expecting the arc of water to get lower and lower until it's just a dribble down his chin.

"What the angel spits up the old man drinks down."

I turn around. There's a licorice man sitting on a park bench a few feet away. That's what I think when I see him, that he's made of licorice. His long, skinny arms are draped over the back of the bench. His long, skinny legs are stretched out in front of him and crossed at the ankles.

The man is white-skinned, but everything else about him is black, from his desert boots to his socks and tight pants to his turtleneck sweater. He's wearing shades and he has black hair and a little black goatee. There is a notebook open on his lap and a pen tucked behind his ear. The pen is black, too. He is watching the placard man closely.

"Do you think *Gob* whispers in his ear?"

I'm not sure if he's talking to me or just to himself. But I do know what he is. He's a beatnik. Most of them live in New York. I saw pictures of them in *Life* magazine. Or maybe he's just a beatnik in training, because he isn't wearing a beret and he doesn't have a set of bongo drums.

His head swings my way and he smiles like a snake on a sunny rock. I can't see his eyes. All I can see is two of me, one in each lens of his dark glasses. I look surprised.

"I call him Dump Orbit," says the beatnik.

I roll Diablo back a wheel turn or two, and from the safety of this new distance I frown at the beatnik.

"You shouldn't call people names." I keep my voice low so that the placard man doesn't hear.

The beatnik gathers in his stringy limbs, wraps his hands around his knees. "So, Startled Blond Boy disapproves. That's cool—speaking out against what's cruel." And he smiles differently now, more kindly. Then he takes the pen from behind his ear and writes something in his notebook. He seems to forget all about me. I edge a bit closer.

"Are you a poet?"

He looks up. His head is kind of dancing around as if he's listening to Harry Belafonte.

"I dabble," he says. "Turn the world into words. Kick the 'ell out of it, if you dig what I mean."

I don't know what he's talking about. So he flips back a few pages in his notebook and holds it up for me to see.

It's a cartoon. In the first frame he has written *WORLD* in big block letters, and there is this tiny cartoon beatnik kicking the letter *L* right out of it. In the next frame, the cartoon beatnik is standing in the space where the *L* used to be, his hands in the air, victorious.

Holy moly.

He's a beatnik and a poet *and* an artist. But now he is writing in his notebook again. I wheel a little closer and a little closer still, until, accidentally, I bump my tire into his foot.

I apologize. He looks up, surprised.

"You still here, SBB?"

SBB? It takes me a minute to figure out what he means. "Why do you call him Dump Orbit?"

The beatnik's head swings back and forth like a cobra dancing to a wooden flute. "You've heard of Sputnik?" he says.

"Everybody's heard of Sputnik." I roll my eyes a bit. "That's the satellite the Russians launched in 1957, three months ahead of the Americans. You can see satellites," I add, since he might not know this. "It's true. They kind of blink."

"Well, SBB, what's going to happen to those blinking tin pots when they run out of steam?"

I haven't thought about this. For one thing, I'm pretty sure satellites don't run on steam.

I shrug. He leans back and stares up and there is a sun in each lens of his glasses.

"They're going to bump them off," he says. "Or bump them *out*—way, way out, Daddy-o. Out of everybody's hair. Turn off the lights and lock the door, circling the earth forevermore. But not so we can see with our eyes, they're making a scrap heap of the skies."

I can hardly believe my ears. "Did you just make that up?"

He closes his notebook, puts his pen behind his ear again. "Sometimes the words come out like that—all dressed up in party clothes."

It's hard to think of satellites getting old. They are the very newest things in the world.

Suddenly, from over by the water fountain, there is a loud burp. The placard man has finished at last. He stands up straight and stretches out his back.

Dump Orbit. For some reason, he looks a bit better now that I'm thinking of him as an out-of-work satellite. It's as if he is someone who used to be famous.

"Why do you think he picked October 23?"

"Who knows?" says the beatnik. "But there was this kook from the U.K. who believes that the world began on October 23."

"Are you kidding?"

"Nope. October 23, 4004 B.C. At noon."

"At noon?"

"Right on the dot," he says, but he's grinning now. "That's what Archbishop Usher wanted all us cats and kittens to believe."

"Who's he?"

"The kook I was telling you about. He lived about three hundred years ago. Figured out when the world began. Don't ask me how he did the math. But by some mighty coincidence—and I mean a coincidence of the intergalactic kind—Dump Orbit over there has picked the exact same date for the world to end."

Just then Dump Orbit bawls something that's so garbled I can hardly tell which language he's speaking. It's just to clear his throat, I guess, because the next thing he says is crystal clear.

"We're all going *BOOM!*"

Out of the corner of my eye I see a little girl get her feet snaggled up in her skipping rope. I see an old woman take hold of her husband's hand. I think of our new house on Clemow Avenue and all I want to do is go home. I look at the beatnik who grins at me like a Cheshire cat.

"As Mr. Lawrence Ferlinghetti says, that man has been 'hung up too long in strange suspenders.' "

SHELTER

That night when Dad comes up to say good night, I ask him about Archbishop Usher.

"Good chap," he says. "Knew him when he was an altar boy. Knew him when he was a pup."

"He lived hundreds of years ago."

"Oh, *that* Archbishop Usher. Never heard of him."

I snuggle down into my bedclothes. "He said the world began on October 23, 4004 B.C. At noon."

My father's brow furrows. "I find that a little hard to believe," he says. "I know for a fact that God takes his lunch break at noon. Used to see him down at the pub. Always ordered the plowman's lunch with an extra pickled egg."

It's very hard to get useful information out of my father. But I don't really care this time. I kind of like the idea of God eating pickled eggs.

Dad gives me a kiss. I give him a hug.

"There's a man in the park who says the world is going to end on the exact same day, October 23."

Dad looks interested. "First I've heard of it," he says. Then he sits up and starts looking for his pipe in his pocket. "There's always someone who thinks the world is coming to an end. I guess they don't have anything to look forward to."

It isn't much of an answer, but it seems true. I bet Dump Orbit doesn't have anything to look forward to. He's so old. What did the beatnik say? "Hung up too long in strange suspenders." I imagine Dump Orbit hanging by his suspenders from a tree waving his sign high above Adams Park for anyone to see if only they looked up.

◎ ◎ ◎

The next morning I race to Buster's place at nine on the dot. There's a dump truck in the driveway. I wonder if it's his father's. Then I remember him saying his dad was a mathematician or something. I can't see what a mathematician would want with a dump truck unless he had a pile of used numbers lying around.

There's a lot of noise coming from the backyard so I don't bother to go to the door. And sure enough, I find Buster and James leaning against the garage. Ga*rage*. I remind myself how to say it.

A front-end loader is digging a huge pit in Buster's backyard. A bunch of workers are standing around leaning on shovels watching, as if the front-end loader is their teacher and they'll start digging as soon as they get the hang of it.

"Are you getting a swimming pool?"

Buster shakes his head. "Way better," he says. "We're getting a bomb shelter. It's going to be so big, we'll be able to stay in it for twelve years."

"Holy moly."

James has his hands deep in his pockets, and he's rocking back and forth. His eyes are slits. I'm not sure if he's angry or thinking hard.

"Just imagine," he says. "No school for twelve years."

"I know," says Buster excitedly. Then his face drops. "My dad says we'll get homeschooled. Seems like a waste of time to me."

I try to imagine my mum and dad as teachers—Mum in her gingham apron with her wooden spoon, Dad in his hard hat with his pipe.

"At least they won't keep asking you what you did at school all day," I say. The boys agree that this is a good point.

"And think of this," says James. "If you *didn't* get homeschooled—if you just played table hockey and read comics and watched TV—then when you came out of the bomb shelter you'd have to go into grade five and you'd be twenty-three years old."

This is a spectacularly important point. You'd think that Buster would be relieved about having to be homeschooled, but instead he looks a little worried.

"If there is a Third World War, will there be any TV?"

"It depends," says James. "If the Yanks win, then it'll probably be all the same stuff. *The Andy Griffith Show, Huckleberry Hound, The Price Is Right*—all the good shows. But if the Russians win . . ."

"Maybe there'll be nothing but shows about soldiers," I suggest.

"Or potatoes," says Buster.

"Or ballet," says James.

And this is the most horrible thought of all. To be stuck underground for twelve years with nothing on TV but ballet.

We watch the workers for a bit, watch as the hole grows bigger and the garden grows smaller and smaller. I try to imagine how many cans of food you'd need to get through twelve years living underground. At home we always have a pantry full of canned food that we never eat. It's because of the Battle of Britain. My mother makes sure we have canned food in case there's another war. Sometimes when my parents are out we open a can or two of ravioli or cabbage rolls. I love it! It's good the same way Wonder Bread is good: sweet and soft. It doesn't shout, "Hey, look at me! Don't I taste great?" Canned food just *is*.

I look at the hole in the garden getting deeper and I try to imagine it filled with loaves of Wonder Bread, enough to last twelve years. I know the bread will last for twelve years—that's why it's called Wonder Bread—but I'm just not sure how many loaves you'd need.

Then I remember another great feature of Wonder Bread. You can squish it really, really small.

"What about *your* family?" Buster asks.

I shrug. "I guess we'll go down to the basement and duck and cover like it says on the posters."

"Okay, but what about after that?"

I shrug again. We haven't talked about building a shelter at my place. I have a feeling Mum would say only common people talk about building bomb shelters.

"We could never build a shelter in our backyard anyway, on account of our dog." The boys look interested. "I mean, the garden is wall-to-wall poop. And besides, he's vicious. Last week he ate a whole lawn chair."

Buster's eyes light up. "That could be useful," he says. "My father says that if they drop the bomb there may be ravenous hordes combing the neighborhood looking for food and shelter."

"Do you have a dog?" I ask Buster.

He shakes his head. "No, but my dad is going to get a gun. Maybe a machine gun. He says he'll teach me how to use it."

"That would be hunky-dory," I say. And then I wonder if I could fool a ravenous horde with my six-shooter. I try to imagine what a ravenous horde would look like. In comic books there are mutants with white glowing eyes and green spit dribbling out of their mouths. Then there are the pod people in *Invasion of the Body Snatchers*.

I don't know how effective Kincho would be against pod people. I don't know how effective a machine gun would be, either, but I don't want to say that. I've only known Buster one day.

I turn to James, who is pretty quiet right now. He's tugging on his spot of gray hair.

"What is your family going to do?" I ask.

He shrugs and his eyes flicker away.

"He doesn't need to worry," says Buster.

James glares at him. I have never had a friend for more than one year but I know that glare. It's the shut-up glare. James looks really mad, and I feel as if it's partly my fault.

"You guys want a Pez?" I ask quickly. I'm already fishing the dispenser out of my jeans pocket. Everybody loves Pez.

"The Creature from the Black Lagoon!" says James. "I've got the Werewolf at home." He looks at me as if this almost makes us blood brothers. I think he's also relieved that I've changed the subject.

Meanwhile, Buster is shoving out his hand. But I hold back. I cover the dispenser with my other hand and make a serious face.

"There's just one thing," I tell them. "This is an enchanted Pez dispenser. When you suck on your Pez capsule, you will travel to another time—any time you so desire."

"The future, too?"

"The future, too."

Buster checks with James as if James is his older brother.

James gently lowers Buster's waiting hand. "I'd better check this out first, buddy. Make sure it's safe."

I click back the Creature from the Black Lagoon's head. Out comes a lemon-yellow Pez. James draws it slowly from the dispenser as if it might be connected by wires to a bomb. He closes his eyes and places the candy on his tongue. He sucks on it and we watch and wait. Then his eyes fly open. He looks around and gasps.

"It works!" he says.

"So where are you?" says Buster.

"I'm in your garden one hundred years from now. And we're *still talking about the stupid bomb shelter!*"

James is making a joke—I know that—but Buster looks put out. Sheesh! I have to think quickly again. "Did you talk to whoever you had to talk to? You know, before you can tell me about what's happening in the park."

James's brow clears. "Yeah," he says. "I almost forgot." He looks at his grownup-looking gold watch. "Whoa, Nelly. They're expecting us right about now." Then he looks directly at me. "They already know you," he says. "Let's go."

SAFE HOUSE

We bike over to Adams Park. Buster and James go right down the steps—a dozen of them—on their bikes, so I have to follow. I'm scared, but there isn't time to get *really* scared and before I know it, I'm at the bottom. Good ol' Diablo.

While we're checking our bikes for damage, I tell Buster and James about Dump Orbit and about meeting the beatnik.

"The old guy's name is Alphonse," says James.

"That's a stupid name," says Buster. "Dump Orbit is better."

"How do you know his name?" I ask James.

"Sometimes they come and get him and take him away. You know, to the funny farm."

I nod. I know what the funny farm is—a hospital for crazy people.

"What about the beatnik?"

"He's creepy," says Buster. "My mother says he's probably a prevert."

"What's that?"

"The kind of guy who likes to get children to sit on his lap."

"You mean a pervert," says James. "Did he try to touch you?"

"Of course not."

"Did he try to get you to go into the woods with him?"

"No."

"But you did go in the woods over there, right?" James points to the trees on the north side. "What were you doing?"

So I start to tell them about the night I was walking Kincho.

"You came down here at *night*?" says James.

"I was walking the dog."

"The one who eats chairs?" says Buster.

I nod.

"And what happened?" asks James, never taking his eyes off me.

"I saw something."

They glance at each other, then back at me. "What kind of something?"

"There was this . . . . this thing."

"Did it growl?"

"Did it attack?"

I nod my head and then shake my head. "It growled, all right, but not at me. There was a girl."

The boys look at each other and nod. Then James says, "You've got to tell this to the council."

"The council?"

But he has already hopped on his bike. "Come on!"

To my surprise, he veers off the path and cuts straight across the lawn toward the hedge that forms the southern boundary of the park.

"You heard him!" says Buster over his shoulder, racing after his friend.

I hop on Diablo and head off in hot pursuit.

James is speeding straight toward the hedge. What's scary is that he isn't slowing down one bit as he gets nearer and nearer. Neither is Buster.

All I can think is that it's some crazy game of chicken—the last one to stop is the winner. I don't stop to think about it—about anything—but pedal for all I'm worth.

Then, to my shock, James hurtles right into the shrubbery and disappears.

Fwoop!

Now Buster's gone, too.

Fwoop!

"Come on, Diablo," I whisper. With my head low and shoulders hunched and—at the last second—my eyes tightly shut, I hit the wall.

Fwoop!

When I open my eyes I half expect to be in some other place—some other time, like *One Step Beyond*. But what I find is a little clearing of dappled light that smells of damp earth and rotten tree stumps. The only sound I can hear is my heart, three times louder than normal.

It's not like the woods on the north side, all overgrown and dense and thorny. There's a narrow path through the trees up the hill. James and Buster are already on it, their legs pumping hard.

I notice there is a whole network of paths. I think of how often over the last month I've walked beside these bushes dragged along by Kincho, never knowing there was a secret world just one green step away.

We come, at last, to another clearing around the base of a tree—a huge oak that reminds me of Popeye showing off his biceps, except the tree has a whole lot more arms. There are two bikes lying there already. Fifteen feet above my head is the biggest tree fort I've ever seen. James and Buster are on the ladder climbing that tree like ants scampering up a lemonade glass.

"Come on!" whispers James, and I follow. James reaches the floor of the fort and knocks three times. A round trap-door opens and he scuttles up and in. He kneels to give Buster a hand, and then Buster turns to help me.

As soon as I'm in, James puts the plug in the hole. Another boy places a heavy stone on top of the trapdoor. He looks up at me as he dusts off his hands.

It's the dark-skinned boy from the other day, the one who warned me not to go into the woods on the other side.

"Hi," he says. "We were expecting you."

There's one other person in the tree fort. A girl. She's sitting cross-legged on the deck with a large scrapbook open on her lap. She looks up at me and her eyes are as blue as the skies over a Paint by Numbers meadow. She's tanned and freckly and blond, except I know the proper name for her hair color from all the Paint by Numbers I've done. It's flaxen and it's tied back in a tight ponytail. She's wearing shorts and no shoes and her legs are as bruised and scratched as a boy's. Her shirt has horses prancing all over it.

Best of all, she has a powder-blue Brownie Starflash camera hanging on a strap around her neck. And it's loaded.

I stare at her and then at Buster and James and again at the other boy. James introduces me. "Rex Zero, this is Sami Karami." I shake his hand, wondering if that's his real name. If it is, it's a great superhero name.

Then James turns to the girl. "And this is Kathy Brown," he says. She looks at me, pushes a strand of hair out of her eyes, but doesn't say anything.

"I saw you before," I say. I pull her flashbulb out of my pocket and hand it to her. She looks surprised and then her brow gets all creased.

"Were you the one with the dog?" I nod and her face clouds over. "Well, your stupid dog scared Tronido," she snaps. "That's why he ran away."

"Pardon me?"

"That's why I didn't get any good pictures." She looks down at the scrapbook and turns it around so I can see.

There are only three snapshots on the page. One is a total blur—a black-and-gray soup. On one of the others you can make out some of the shrubbery and two eyes. The last snapshot looks like it's a picture of something alive—something large and black—but it's hard to say where the animal leaves off and the bush begins.

"I almost had him," she says. "Then you came along."

I keep looking at the pictures even though there is nothing much to see. I'm too mad to look at Kathy, too mad to speak. Who does she think she is, blaming me for showing up? I swallow hard. Then I get to my feet and glance at James and Buster, then at Sami.

"Well?" she says. It sounds like an accusation.

I head over to the north wall of the tree fort. The walls have sticks pointing out at angles all around. They're old hockey sticks without the blades and with the ends sharpened to a point.

This tree fort is a stronghold and I'm still not sure against what. Maybe that thing Kathy was trying to photograph. The thing she blames *me* for scaring away! I can feel everyone's eyes on me.

Finally, Buster comes over and speaks in my ear quietly. "She can be pretty bossy, but she's okay," he says. "Say something."

I look out across the hockey-stick ramparts and imagine the foliage is a thousand tiny paint-by-number sections. I try to count the number of colors I'd need to paint it. It helps to calm me down.

"Sorry," I say, though I can hardly get it out. "But you took three pictures before me and my dog even got there."

"I heard you coming."

"No, you didn't."

"Well, *he* did. Tronido did. You think he can't smell a dog? That's why he was so edgy." Her voice is raised and the others move away a bit, even though she is still just sitting there, cross-legged. "This time I could have had him," she says. "One really good photo is all we need to prove it. To prove it to the grownups. But you showed up and ruined everything."

I look at the others, who seem kind of shocked and embarrassed.

I just want to run away. Back to the House of Punch. Back to Vancouver. The only thing is, I'll have to pass Kathy Brown, who looks as mad as a wasp on flypaper. Who knows what she'll do?

"What is it? Some wild dog or something?"

"Hah!" says Kathy, her voice getting louder. "A wild dog we could catch. There's no way we could catch Tronido. That's why I have to photograph him. We need proof."

I'm completely confused. "Listen. I'm new here. I didn't know what I was doing. I'm sorry if I wrecked things." I know I don't really sound sorry but I don't care.

Then I realize she's crying. Kathy is crying. Holy moly.

"Nobody believes us," she says. "It's out there ready to kill us and they don't even care!"

I walk over to her and sit down, cross-legged, in front of her. I pull the ball of hair from my pocket and hold it out.

Her shoulders stop shaking. She sniffs. The others move over to join us.

Soon we are all sitting in a ragged circle. James finds a handkerchief and gives it to Kathy. I can't believe it—a real handkerchief with *JS* monogrammed in the corner.

Kathy sniffs again and rubs her nose with the handkerchief. She sits up straighter. She reaches out to touch the fur. Then she looks at me—looks at my whole face as if it has writing all over it and she's trying to read what it says. She wipes her eyes with the handkerchief and looks again. I put the fur in her hand.

"This isn't from your dog, is it?" she asks.

"I went back the next morning. I found it near where I found your flashbulb." She cradles it as if it were a gerbil or a baby bird.

"Was that the morning we saw you?" Sami asks. I nod. "We were keeping an extra lookout," he says. "Because Kathy told us what happened. It was only the second sighting this month. For a while there, we thought maybe Tronido was gone."

"Please . . . will someone tell me who Tronido is?"

"I wish you'd seen him," says Kathy, ignoring my question. She sounds a little desperate.

71

"I did."

That gets her attention. "Really?"

"After you took off. He came out . . . well, just part of him. Just for a second. I saw his head and shoulder, that's all."

The others murmur excitedly. But I keep my eyes on Kathy. I gave her back her flashbulb and I gave her the hank of hair, but I want to give her something else.

"It was really brave, what you did. I'm sorry Kincho and I wrecked it."

It feels weird to apologize when only a few minutes earlier I was ready to bop her over the head. But I'm glad I do it. She rubs her face with her hands, blows her nose, and looks a lot better when she looks at me again. She even smiles a bit.

"It's okay," she says. "At least you saw him. That's the important thing."

"But *what* did I see? *Who is Tronido?*"

"A panther," says Kathy Brown. "An escaped panther."

My mouth goes dry. A cat? Of course! Kincho knew all along! He hates cats.

"Don't they live in South America?"

Kathy closes the scrapbook and hands it over, turning it to face me. On the cover is an amazing photograph of a panther staring directly out at me.

"Holy moly," I whisper.

"That's not Tronido," says James, who is leaning over my shoulder. "That's from *National Geographic*."

I turn the page as if I'm opening the Holy Bible. And there, in the center of the next page, is a black-and-white snapshot with crinkly edges, just like the others, but much better. There's a wreath of leaves around the edges but it's dark in the center.

And there *is* something there, something with glowing eyes. A ghostly shape lost amid the twigs and shadows staring out at the photographer, one wicked paw raised. Underneath the snapshot someone has written in ballpoint pen:

Tronido

picture by Kathy Brown
Around 11:00 p.m., May 20, 1962
Adams Park, Ottawa

"Tronido," I say.

"It means 'thunderclap,' " says Kathy as she turns the page for me. There is a newspaper cutting featuring another picture of a panther. I stare at the headline, CAT ON THE LOOSE! Finally, I get around to reading the article but I can't concentrate properly. My mind is racing. All I can grasp is that Tronido escaped from the Granby Zoo, wherever that is.

Then I notice the date. It was more than two years ago.

I'm just about to say something about that, but Kathy turns the page again. There's another newspaper clipping, TRONIDO STILL ON THE LOOSE! This time the article is about a dead cow and how the markings look like it might be the work of "Granby's famous feline fugitive." There have been other sightings: Saint-Rémi, Iberville, Lachute. I don't know where any of these places are, but none of them is Ottawa. "People are warned to keep an eye out," says the article. "Do not leave children unattended." There is a phone number to call if you spot anything suspicious.

"So did you call?" I ask.

"Every time," says Sami, making a sour face. "Nobody ever does a thing."

"Did they see this?" I ask, flipping back to the snapshot.

He nods again wearily. "Of course. The cops came and looked around, told us it was nothing. Same with the SPCA. We even went to the radio station, but they couldn't care less. You know what it's like."

I nod slowly. I do know. Adults hardly ever listen to kids. I turn the page. Another headline, STILL NO TRONIDO. The date on this one is from last fall—less than a year ago. There have been sightings in Montebello and Cumberland. More mutilated livestock.

There is a map in the scrapbook. Granby is in Quebec, south of Montreal, which is a long way away. But every place mentioned in the articles is nearer and nearer to Ottawa. Cumberland is only a few miles away.

A bell rings. We all look up. Far above us, in the topmost limb of the oak tree, there is another boy I hadn't even no-ticed, straddling a branch looking out over Adams Park through a pair of binoculars. He's got a handbell.

Sami stands and cups his hands. "A sighting, Walli?"

Walli sits up, with his legs wrapped tightly around the branch like he's an Indian buffalo hunter. He looks down and shakes his head. "Just some little kid wandering into the bushes looking for his ball."

"We'd better go and check it out," Sami says.

Kathy takes the scrapbook and places it in a metal rubbish tin—garbage can, I mean—standing in the corner of the fort. We leave the stronghold one by one. When we're on the ground again, Sami and James walk their bikes down the hill toward the shrubbery that divides the park from this secret other world.

Immediately, Buster leans close to me. "You know when we were talking about the bomb shelter and James got so . . . you know, shirty?" I don't know what *shirty* means but I remember the shut-up glare James gave Buster. "Well, he's just a bit embarrassed about it because of his dad being a Big Cheese and all."

"A Big Cheese?"

"Yeah. His father's one of the Inner Circle." Buster glances down the hill to check if James has heard us, but James is deep in conversation with Sami. "The Bigwigs," Buster says. "They've got a Special Place for the Bigwigs. *The Government.*"

Now I get it. He means like the War Room, where Winston Churchill met with his generals night and day, even as the bombs were dropping overhead on London in World

War II and people like my mum were eating canned food underground in air-raid shelters.

"Holy moly," I murmur. And Buster looks pleased with himself. I nudge him. "Thanks," I whisper. "I won't say anything."

"Just thought you'd want to know," he says. Then he tromps down the hill to join the boys. But I wait for Kathy, who is only just leaving the fort. She pulls the cover in place and then makes her way down the ladder so fast I almost think she's falling. She drops the last few feet and lands perfectly balanced beside me.

"I'm sorry for . . . for what happened," she says.

"It's okay," I say. The bell is ringing again. "What about all those old people and mothers and kids?" I say.

She shrugs. "There's nothing we can do. We tried to warn them but we gave up. One woman yelled at me." I shake my head. "You can't make people believe what they don't want to believe," she says. Then she tosses me a little smile and heads off down the hill, her Brownie Starflash swinging.

I lean against the oak and think about the smile she tossed me. It makes me think of the shiny surprises they put in a cereal box—decoder rings and dinosaurs. You have to eat a lot of cereal to get one, but it makes your morning if you're lucky enough to be the one who does.

JOHNNY FEDORA AND ALICE BLUE BONNET

When I get home there's just Mum at the stove, Harry Belafonte singing the "Banana Boat Song" on the hi-fi, and Annie Oakley sitting at the kitchen table cutting up a *Glamour* magazine. She's probably going to use the cut-out girls for target practice.

I tell them about Tronido.

"That's stupid," says Annie Oakley.

"It's true," I tell her. "That's what the *thing* was I saw. A panther."

"Are you sure it wasn't the Big Bad Wolf come to eat the bad little boys and girls?"

"Oh, really," says Mum. "Is that necessary?" She sounds like she's saying that getting yourself eaten is the kind of thing only common people would do.

I stare at Annie Oakley. "Why don't you believe me?"

"Panther, my foot!" she snaps. "That's just some fairy tale."

"What about mutants?"

She shakes her scissors in my face. "Mutants are real," she says. "Read the newspaper."

"Annie," says Mum. "Put down those scissors before you poke somebody's eye out."

Annie groans, smashes the scissors down on the table, and stomps out of the kitchen.

◎ ◎ ◎

At dinner we talk about Buster's bomb shelter. Cassiopeia says that now that she's working at Birks Jewelers she will obviously be invited to stay in the Birks' family shelter. She thinks it's in the vault deep under the store on Sparks Street where they keep the gold. Her eyes glitter at the thought of it.

"Nonsense," says my father.

"More peas, anyone?" says Mum.

Letitia says that she thinks Buster's older brother Clem is dishy and she hopes to marry him.

"You're only sixteen," says Cassiopeia.

"One day, I mean," says Letitia. "Then the Keatons will absolutely have to let me stay with them in their shelter for the length of the nuclear winter." She says "nuclear winter" as if it's something cozy—like the last scene in *White Christmas*.

"Clem?" says Mum. "You actually know a boy named Clem?"

"Clement," sighs Letitia, and the rhinestones in the corners of her glasses flash like real jewels.

"My goodness," says Mum, as if she'd better put more potatoes on to boil. But I don't think Letitia has even met Clem, because Buster told me he's away on a canoe trip.

Then Annie Oakley says that she heard the safest place to be in a nuclear war is in a can of tomato soup.

"In a what?" asks Father.

"They've done tests to prove it," says Annie Oakley.

Dad laughs out loud, his Royal Engineers' laugh. "Tomato soup?" he says. "Not cream of mushroom? Split pea? Scotch broth?"

We all laugh, even Annie, but when she catches my eye she sticks her tongue out at me.

"I'll snip that off, young lady," says Mum, and we all laugh again, except for the Sausage. He looks worried. He's digging a crater in his mashed potatoes and piling everything into it: peas and carrots and cut-up bits of pork chop, as if he needs to put them somewhere before this thing happens, whatever it is.

Flora Bella doesn't have anything to say about the bomb shelter. She's looking jaunty in a crown she made out of a *Life* magazine cover and she's got this familiar glint in her eye.

I try not to look at her. I know she's going to get me. And I know I won't be able to resist.

"There isn't going to be a war," says my father, wiping his lips with his napkin. "This fallout-shelter craze is so much stuff and nonsense."

"There, you see," says Mum, as if she's been telling us all along and now it's finally been proven. "Carrots, anyone?"

Annie Oakley says, "I saw the place where the Mounties surrounded that spy. You know, the one who sold Russian secrets to the Americans? Or was it American secrets to the Russians? Anyway, it's on Somerset Street right beside the movie theater where *The Young Lions* is playing."

Letitia sighs again. "I love Marlon Brando as a blond."

"Igor Something," says Annie Oakley. "Igor Stravinsky?"

"Gouzenko," says Father.

"Gesundheit," says Mum.

"EEEEGGGOOR," says Flora Bella, so loudly I drop my knife.

The Sausage starts to whimper.

"YEESSS, MASTER," I say to Flora Bella, my zombie voice wavering, my zombie arms sticking out. Her crown tilts crazily forward, her eyes glow like fog lights. She *is* the master. And just to make sure, she puts a gob of mashed potato on her nose. Now she is utterly irresistible. She leans across her dinner plate and, like Svengali, the famous hypnotizer, she puts me in the Funny Spell.

"Johnny Fedora and Alice Blue Bonnet," she sings in her spookiest voice. I start giggling right away. "Down at the department store."

"No singing at the table," says Mum.

"Wan' another piece of apple pie?" says Flora Bella, making her face into a sun with radiant fingers.

Now I drop my fork as well, which clatters on the plate.

"Oh, not this again," says Dad, throwing down his napkin.

"Been to Texas, Mister Blister Twister?" says Flora Bella.

By now I'm doubling over. Flora Bella is cracking up, too.

"Children," says Mum.

"MUD!" cries Flora Bella, standing on her chair and waving her hands in the air. "It's everywhere, it's everywhere!"

And I'm done for. I'm dimly aware of the others watching: Cassiopeia with her arms crossed in disdain, Letitia with a cross-eyed understanding smile, Annie Oakley snarling. She still doesn't think we should be allowed to sit at the grownup table.

"I don't get it," says the Sausage. He looks ready to cry.

Which is when Flora Bella delivers the *coup de grâce*. "What's so smelly 'bout oooooold jelly!" she says, and her face looks just like Frankenstein's monster.

Now we're both done for. We collapse. We spill out of our chairs like two knocked-over glasses of milk and pool on the floor under the table.

"Oh, good grief!" says Father.

"Get up this instant!" says Mum. "Or there'll be no pudding."

But by now dessert is out of the question. My stomach aches from laughing, I'm gulping for air. Flora Bella's in the same bad way.

It happens every time. Sometimes I'll be alone, just walking down the street, and I *think* the words "Johnny Fedora and Alice Blue Bonnet," and I start laughing all by myself. I have no idea why. It's as if Flora Bella and I, like mad scientists, figured out how to unleash the hidden power in the nucleus of those words from a song we heard on a Disney cartoon. We've smashed the joke atom, and now even the simplest of words is dangerously funny.

We've smashed the joke atom, and now we have to live with the consequences.

THE DIEFENBUNKER

he next day is Sunday. I'm not sure how that happened. It kind of snuck up on me.

We're not allowed to go out on Sunday—at least not to play. Which is weird because we're not religious. Mum says we're Christians but she also says it would be common to talk about it all the time and bore people. I'm not sure we really are Christians. We don't go to church. We don't say grace. We don't have any pictures of Jesus on the walls. I once saw a Paint by Numbers Jesus but my mother wouldn't let me buy it so I bought a man-o'-war instead.

My family can't even play together *inside* on Sundays. Especially not cards. "No cards on Sunday!" says Mum, and I don't get it because we never play cards anyway. I don't think we have a pack in the house.

On Sunday we have three rituals. First, Dad makes a proper English breakfast, which means fried eggs and fried bacon and fried tomatoes and fried sausages and fried mushrooms and fried bread and fried porridge and fried oranges and fried model airplanes. Ritual number two is that we read or play quietly by ourselves in our rooms for hours with no arguing or laughing. Then, finally, there is dreaded ritual number three. We all climb into the Pontiac for a nice drive in the country or to look at the rich people's houses in Rockliffe Park. Mum thinks of the drive as exercise.

I hoped that maybe things would change when we moved east. I thought staying in on Sunday was something that only people in British Columbia did—maybe because of all the rain.

I lie in my room under the sloping ceiling with *The Mountain of Adventure* open on my belly. Philip, Dinah, Jack, and Lucy-Ann are in the Welsh mountains. They're always going somewhere exciting. This time, there are ferocious canines. I picture Kincho. I'm guessing that the mountain is hollow and that people are doing bad things in it that the four adventurers will have to stop.

Apart from getting grownups to do what you want them to do, what I like best about Enid Blyton books is the food. The fabulous four are always packing great picnics. They can have all the canned food they want. But I guess they have to keep up their energy for all those adventures.

I don't bother checking the window today. I'm pretty sure the library police get Sundays off. There may be Communists out there, because I know *they're* not Christians, but there are usually more people out on the street on Sunday, so it's pretty hard to pick the Commies out. If those people on the street are Christians, they're not the same kind of Christians we are. We're stay-at-home Christians.

One thing that's good about today is that it is exactly one week until my birthday. I'll be eleven for real. So what if the Berlin crisis is getting worse every day? Not everything is awful. Dad showed me a picture of a new kind of communications satellite that one day would provide all-day television around the world. So what if the Reds are testing the atomic bomb again? Dad says we can go to the Star Top Drive-in to see John Wayne in *The Comancheros* for my party. As a special treat I might be able to ask a friend along. I'm hoping I can ask two or three. Maybe five!

New friends. And a mystery to solve. It's just like an Enid Blyton. It could be called *The Park of Adventure*.

Suddenly I jump up and run to the window. I scan every yard, every driveway, every branch of every tree. That's where I am when Flora Bella arrives wearing a blue polka-dot dress.

"Isn't it beautiful?" she says. "I'm naming every single polka dot."

"Big deal. I'm looking for a giant killer panther. It ate a cow."

"Really?" she says, and climbs up on my desk to stare out at the sunshiny street. "If it ate a whole cow, do you think it could eat a car?"

I frown. "I don't think panthers are *carivores*."

She sticks out her lower lip. "Too bad. Because then we

85

wouldn't have to go for a family drive. Oh!" she says. "That's what I was supposed to tell you. It's time to go."

◉ ◉ ◉

We head west on Highway 17. The Trans-Canada. Maybe we're going back to Vancouver. I try to imagine being stuck in the Pontiac for three days with four sisters and one brother and two parents. Kincho is too big and too dangerous to take with us. One Sunday he saw a cat and tried to jump out the window to get it. He tore Cassiopeia's dress and we had to go home. Another time, we stopped for ice cream and he ate the Sausage's, threw up in the car, and we had to go home. That was the last time he came, which is kind of too bad, because whenever he was along, the trips were a lot shorter.

As we head out of town I realize that it took three days to get here from Vancouver by train, and the train traveled day and night, so it would be more like six days—maybe more— by car. It's so hot I feel like I'm melting along all my edges. I'm sharing the backseat with Annie Oakley on my left and Letitia and Cassiopeia on my right. What if their edges are melting, too? What if we all fuse together and become Siamese quadruplets?

We drive through somewhere named Carp, but when we stop for gas the attendant pronounces it "Kayrp." Whatever place it is, there is nothing to look at. But you wouldn't know that to hear my mother.

"Oh, look at the lovely silo," she says. "My, my, what a fine-looking silo. See the silo, children?"

We all look up way too late to see anything she points to. Cassiopeia and Letitia are looking at the pictures in *Glamour* and Annie Oakley is carving a knife out of a piece of wood. I'm reading *The Mountain of Adventure*. Flora Bella is in the front seat between Dad and Mum, still naming the polka dots on her dress: "Della, Mordella, Prudella, Fondella . . ." Her voice drones on. The Sausage is asleep on Mum's lap, with his thumb in his mouth.

Then, just as Philip, Dinah, Jack, and Lucy-Ann are being led at gunpoint to the legendary King of the Mountains, the Pontiac pulls over to the side of the road. I look nervously through the back window, half expecting to see Gypsies with guns. Then I remember we're not in the Welsh mountains and I look for cops.

Maybe Dad was speeding. Maybe you're not allowed to have eight people in a car.

But there are no cops. There is nothing. Just fields whichever way you look.

The rest of the family is looking up from their magazines and knives and polka dots.

"Where are we?" says Flora Bella.

Sometimes when it's hot, we'll stop for a soda pop, but

there isn't any pop around here. My father rolls down his window and points with his pipe out at the field just across the way. When I sit up and look more closely, I realize it's not an ordinary field at all. There's a radio tower and these metal mushrooms the size of garbage cans sticking up out of the ground. There's also a barbed-wire fence stretching as far as I can see.

"Remember last night's discussion?" he asks.

"About bomb shelters?" asks Annie Oakley. "Do we have one, too? Is this where it is?"

"You're partially right," he says. "There *is* a shelter—but it's not for the likes of us."

Annie Oakley flops back in her seat, annoyed.

"It's the biggest shelter in the country, a huge complex, ninety feet underground with ceilings of concrete five feet thick," says my father. *The Field of Adventure*, I think, which doesn't sound very exciting. "They've nicknamed it the Diefen-bunker."

"Why?" I ask.

"Because of the prime minister," says Annie Oakley.

"We have a prime minister named Diefenbunker?"

Everybody laughs, even Flora Bella, who doesn't even know what a prime minister is. The only one not laughing is the Sausage because he's still asleep.

"The prime minister's name is Diefen*baker*," says my father. "Don't they teach you anything in school?" Dad is leaning his arm on the car door, staring out at the field. "It's been quite the undertaking. There's a war cabinet room, of course, the emergency operations center, the Bank of Canada vault. Oh, and the CBC is there, too."

So, that's one good thing. There *will* be TV after they drop the bomb. I can't wait to tell James and Buster. But I hope it's not only Canadian TV. Canadian TV is mostly people playing fiddles or *Front Page Challenge*. That's a quiz show where people in bow ties try to guess who the famous person is standing right behind them. It's never a movie star. It's always someone who invented a new kind of screwdriver or proved that you can grow turnips under your bed.

My father is going on about how amazing the secret bunker is when suddenly I remember what Buster told me about James's father.

This must be it!

"Dad?" I ask, leaning my chin on the back of his seat. "Is it just for Big Cheeses?"

"Exactly," he says. *"Les Grands Fromages."*

"Then, how do you know about it?"

He turns just enough to catch my eye. He raises his eyebrow and, for one moment, manages to look truly shady.

"Oh, stop playing," says Mum, and pokes him affectionately in the arm.

The car has grown dead silent. So silent you can hear the grasshoppers chirping in the tall yellow grass and a crow complaining somewhere.

We are all waiting. And because we are waiting, my

father does what he always does. He starts fooling around with his pipe.

"Dad!" says Annie Oakley. She looks like she's ready to stab him in the head with her brand-new wooden knife.

"Are you a spy?" I ask, hoping beyond hope that it's true.

"Are you a friend of the prime minister's?" asks Cassiopeia.

"Where are we?" says the Sausage, who has just woken up.

My father raises his hands. "All right, all right," he says. "My company helped build the thing. It was before I got here, of course. It was mostly up and running last year. There's still some work going on, but the bunker is already operational in a hush-hush kind of way." He chuckles. "Well, not all that hush-hush. The *Toronto Star* flew a plane over the site when they were building it, and the next day the whole country knew about it."

I look out at the field. I imagine the prime minister and the head of the bank and the panelists on *Front Page Challenge* all walking around underground talking very, very quietly. A hawk is circling high above. I wish I could see what he sees. I sure can't see much from down here.

Then a bad thought occurs to me.

"You didn't see the plans, did you?"

"No, it was all pretty well finished before I came onboard."

I let out a sigh of relief. "Because, if you had seen the secret plans, they'd have to kill you, right?"

"Hadn't really thought of it," says Dad, flashing me a smile in the rearview mirror. "Well, shall we be off, then?" He reaches down to turn the ignition key. The car throbs back to life.

I can't wait to let my new friends in on this. Once I've told James, then he'll be able to tell me himself about moving into the Diefenbunker in case of a nuclear war. And he'll know that my dad, while he's not exactly a Big Cheese, is the kind of man who works for a company that makes the world a safer place for Big Cheeses.

Dad turns the car around, which takes five attempts, and then we head home. He closes his window and the car seems stuffier than ever. I try to make myself more comfortable and Annie Oakley gives me a sharp elbow in the side.

"Owww!" I'm just about to complain to Mum when I see the storm in Annie's eyes. She looks much angrier than she could possibly be with just me. She's angry a lot of the time, but when I look more closely, I see something else. Something I've *never* seen in Annie Oakley's face before.

She looks scared.

"What's the matter?" I ask, leaning close for her to whisper her answer in my ear.

Except she doesn't whisper, she screams.

"Owww!"

I cover my ear. The car wobbles as if maybe the scream broke the axle.

"Did we hit something?" says Dad.

"How can he be so *happy*?" shouts Annie Oakley. Her voice stabs the air and her new knife stabs the back of the driver's seat.

I glance at Letitia and Cassiopeia, who are looking past me at Annie Oakley. "He who?" they say.

"How can he be so 'Oh, isn't it *amazing*' and 'Oh, isn't it so *great*'?"

Everyone is very quiet, everyone except Annie Oakley.

"*He* seems to have forgotten that *he* said there wasn't going to *be* a war. Just yesterday!"

The air inside the car is getting thinner, as if Annie Oakley has punched a hole right through to some other place and all the air is draining out into there.

"It's just a *craze*. It's all *stuff and nonsense*. Blah, blah, blah, blah."

"What are you talking about, dear?" says Mum.

"About him!" says Annie, shoving her knife into the back of Dad's seat again. "*He* is a big, fat *liar*!"

Finally, I get it.

This would usually be the point when Mum would suggest stopping for a lovely ice cream cone. But she doesn't. Like all of us, her eyes drift to the man behind the wheel. He removes the pipe from his clenched teeth.

"You needn't worry, darling," he says calmly. "I meant

what I said yesterday. There won't be any war. Cooler heads will prevail."

"There, you see?" says Mum. She turns to us with a tin of toffees. "Sweets, anyone?"

Flora Bella and I take about six each because Mum isn't watching us. She's looking anxiously at Annie Oakley, but Annie isn't looking back.

"War or no war, it's important that preparations are made," says Dad. "Just in case. An ounce of prevention is worth a pound of cure and all that."

Cautiously I turn to glance at Annie Oakley. Her head has sunk between her shoulder blades, but her eyes are still on fire. It feels like it's going to be World War III right here in the Pontiac. She reminds me of a snapping turtle and I lean away from her.

Dad shifts the rearview mirror so that he can see Annie.

"Sweetheart," he says, just to her eyes, "if I didn't believe we could avoid this nonsense, I'd be forced to think that everything we went through in the last war was a complete and utter waste of time. I can't really believe that."

The car becomes deathly quiet. I look sideways. Annie sniffs and crosses her arms and looks out the window. I think there is a tear in her eye. If there is, it must be a very brave tear to venture into such a dangerous place.

Then I think how weird it is that in two days I've seen two brave girls cry.

ALONE AGAIN

When I arrive at Buster's the next morning, his dad is standing in the driveway watching the workers. Buster's father has a flattop like Buster's and his hair is red, just a more weary shade of red. He is wearing a checkered shirt and a tie with numbers painted on it. I wonder if all mathematicians wear ties with numbers on them, kind of like a uniform.

The workmen are putting in the forms for pouring concrete. I know that's what they're doing because I've gone on job sites with my father.

"Cement truck coming today, sir?"

He looks at me. "Haven't seen you around before," he says.

"We just moved here. I'm a friend of Buster's."

"Buster?"

I can't remember Buster's real name. Luckily, Mr. Keaton puts two and two together.

"Kevin," he says.

"Right, Kevin." I introduce myself and shake his hand. I'm pretty good at knowing what to do with grownups. When you move a lot it's an important skill to learn.

"Is Bus—I mean, is Kevin up yet?"

He frowns again. "Kevin?"

"Your son."

"Yes, I know who he is," he says. "But he's gone."

I go cold all over. "Gone, sir?"

"Up north with Mrs. Keaton. Up to her folks' place in Wakefield for a bit of a getaway."

"Oh." I'm relieved he's not dead. But I'm still kind of shocked. Maybe he phoned me when we were out on our drive. Or maybe he didn't because our number isn't in the book yet.

"When will he be back, sir?"

He sighs. "Well, I'll tell you, sonny. He'll be back when he's had a chance to do some serious thinking." That sounds ominous. It's hard to think of Buster doing much serious thinking. "He started up at the dinner table the other night about some wildcat loose in the neighborhood. Said he'd seen it himself. That's why I've sent him up-country for a bit."

"Where he'll be safe," I say.

Now Mr. Keaton looks downright angry. "Tarnation!" he says. "I don't know about your parents, but we don't have much patience with cockamamie tales in the Keaton household. There's enough *real* danger around, what with the Reds threatening world domination."

"Yes, sir."

"Who spreads these rumors anyway?" he asks. I'm not sure if he means about the Reds or the panthers. "Well, Kevin's not going to hear such nonsense up at his Grandmother McGregor's. Now, there's a woman who has no time for a runaway imagination."

I don't know what to say. I thank Mr. Keaton, because you have to be polite to grownups, even crazy ones. As I ride away on Diablo I try to imagine living in a bomb shelter with Mr. Keaton for twelve years. Yikes! I'd rather take my chances with the mutants.

James answers my knock at his front door. I smile, relieved to see him, but then my smile slips. "What's wrong?" I ask.

He looks down and kicks at the welcome mat with the toe of his running shoe.

"You don't have to tell me," I say quickly, because I have this horrible feeling he's got some really bad news.

"It's okay," he says. Then he glances back into the house to see if anyone is there. There is only a white Persian cat sitting dead center on the hall carpet. The carpet is Persian, too. Imagine that. The cat doesn't look as if it's listening to us, but you can never tell with cats.

"We had a fight," he says. "My father and mother and me." He checks again. "They want to send me away to school."

"Oh," I say. "It's no fair having a fight with your parents, because there's two of them."

He tugs at his little patch of gray hair. "Not this time. They both want me to go away to school but not the same school, so they were fighting each other, too. Mom wants me to go to Ashbury. But Dad wants me to go to some other place. Somewhere safe."

"Isn't Ashbury safe?"

He shrugs and his eyes skitter away from mine. "It's a good school, I guess, but Dad doesn't want me to even be in Ottawa in case . . . in case, you know . . ."

I do know. But I still don't understand. "I saw the Diefenbunker yesterday," I tell him. "I mean, I saw where it was. If there was a war, you'd be safer there than anywhere in the whole country, wouldn't you?"

He looks at me as if I'm an alien.

I should shut up because I'm giving away Buster's secret, but I can't help myself. "Well, I thought your dad, being a Big Cheese and all . . ."

"Buster," James groans. "He is such a moron."

"Sorry," I say. "I just thought . . . Sorry."

James looks back at the cat, who pretends to be licking itself. Then he steps out onto the front porch and quietly pulls the door shut behind him. "I shouldn't have said that about Buster," he says. "It's just that he gets muddled sometimes. Maybe you noticed. My dad is the head of Central Mortgage and Housing."

"What's that?" I ask.

He shrugs. "I don't know. But for some reason, he's one of the people who gets to go to the Diefenbunker. He even has a little office there. Except, he's not going to go."

"What?"

James shakes his head. "Dad says not even the prime minister is going to go."

"I don't get it."

"Diefenbaker. The place is named after him but he won't even go and look inside it. You know why?"

I shake my head.

"Well, it's the same reason my dad won't go. Because he can't take his family with him. Not even my mom can go."

"And Mrs. Diefenbaker can't go?"

He shakes his head. "The place is huge, but it only holds five hundred people and there's no room for family."

I can't believe it. No room for family? "God, it would be horrible to be separated from your dad for years."

That's when James laughs. It's kind of a firecracker laugh—over in a second. "Days, you mean. There are going to be enough provisions for thirty days. That's all."

"But Buster said—"

"Thirty *days*," repeats James.

I stare at him and I can see it in his eyes. This is the real truth. There are a whole bunch of different kinds of truth, but this is the real one.

KATHY BROWN

don't ride down the steps into Adams Park. There's no one to keep up with, no one to show off to. I look around for Dump Orbit or the beatnik poet. They're not there. I stand tall in the saddle and cast my eyes all the way to the arched tunnel that passes under Bank Street. I'm looking for Sami or Kathy, but it's just like before. Nothing. Just mothers and baby buggies, mothers and baby buggies, as far as the eye can see. They're all clustered around the fountain fanning their babies. It's the hottest day yet.

The trapdoor to the tree fort isn't closed. I poke my head through the hole. Kathy is sitting there, leaning against the wall with her Brownie around her neck, writing something in the scrapbook.

"Shouldn't you close the trapdoor?" I say. "What if I was the panther?"

"Panthers don't ride Raleigh three-speeds," she says

without looking up. She smiles a little to herself. With her right hand she works a knot free from the plank next to her leg. The knot is about two inches across and the hole is directly above where Diablo lies below.

A spy hole. I'm impressed. She plugs the knothole up again without looking at me.

I'm still standing on the ladder, not sure whether I should wait for an invitation to come in. I wipe my forehead on my shirtsleeve. I'm all sticky. I rest my arms on the floor and rest my chin on my arms. "So, what kind of bikes *do* panthers ride?" I ask.

"They don't," she says. "Tronido escaped from a zoo, not a circus, Rex Zero." I like the way she says my whole name even though she sounds sarcastic. She stops writing and closes the book. Finally, she looks at me. "Are you coming in or not?"

I climb inside, lower the trapdoor, and crawl to the other wall, across from her.

"Did you hear about James?" I ask her. She hasn't, so I tell her, and it makes me feel as if I'm really one of the gang.

"How could they do something like that?"

I shrug. "I guess they just want to be sure he's safe."

"That's stupid," she says. "There isn't going to be a war."

She sounds so confident it makes me feel a little better. Then I tell her about Buster.

"You see what Tronido is doing?" she says. "He's making

everybody's life miserable. Somebody has got to do something."

She's right. There's nothing we can do about the bomb, but maybe—just maybe—we can do something about the panther.

"We should try to catch him." It's out before I know what I'm saying.

She looks up and her forehead is puckered like a prune. "Are you kidding?" she says. "He weighs a hundred and twenty pounds. He can bring down a cow."

"I know, but we're not cows. I mean, cows don't have ideas. Cows don't have weapons."

She rolls her eyes. "So what do you suggest? We set up a Heffalump Trap like Winnie-the-Pooh?"

"Maybe we could find a cow and use it as bait?"

She is about to argue with me when she realizes I'm kidding. "Okay," she says. "You go find a cow. And I'll find a big net."

"Or we could throw a bucket of water on him and watch him melt."

Her smile is a thing of beauty.

"Want a Pez?" I ask. I get out my dispenser. She asks to look at it. "It's the Creature from the Black Lagoon."

She nods. "I was just thinking how weird it is to eat something that a monster coughs up in your hand."

"What we really need is a bottle of cream soda," I say.

"What? You think panthers like cream soda?"

It's funny, because I was thinking about how hot it was, but she never stopped thinking about Tronido. "I meant us. Come on. It's my treat," I say.

We go to the Clemow Smoke Shop. Mr. Papazian looks glad to see me.

"So you found a friend," he says.

I'm embarrassed, but Kathy doesn't seem to care. I get one pop bottle and wipe it off with the rag that hangs by the cooler. She gets two straws while I open the bottle. She doesn't have a bike so I have to walk Diablo, but he doesn't mind.

We start up Bank Street. She is chatting away now and she sounds different. I'm not sure how, but I like her voice. She talks about her class at Mutchmor and about her mom, but not about her dad. I don't ask. As we pass Gladstone Avenue she points west.

"I live down there," she says. Then she talks about basketball. She doesn't just sound different, she's like a whole different person. It's as if she's been let out of a cage.

Suddenly I realize she's talking about going swimming at some place called the Shadow and I ask her what that's like. I'm imagining an underground cavern like the Diefenbunker—and swimming ninety feet below the ground from room to room.

"It costs a quarter and there's too much chlorine, but it's okay," she says.

It turns out it's not a swimming hole at all. It's the *Château*, the Château Laurier, which is a hotel.

"We stayed there when we first got to Ottawa because our house wasn't ready for us," I tell her.

"You *lived* at the Shadow?"

"For a whole week. I didn't even know there was a swimming pool. But there was this cafeteria in the basement where you could take anything you wanted from behind glass doors, and I had a chocolate éclair at every meal: breakfast, lunch, and dinner."

She is staring at me. "Are you rich?" she asks.

I shrug my shoulders. "Sometimes." And I tell her a little about my family, about being on our feet sometimes and then being off our feet again.

Then I tell her something I never tell anyone, about the time when my dad had an accident and we had to live in a basement—all eight of us—and my mother hung up sheets for walls and all we ate was boiled celery.

"Is it any good?" she asks.

"No." She looks sad. "It's okay," I tell her. "My dad got better and we're rich again. Now we can afford celery *and* Cheez Whiz."

She looks as if she's going to say something but changes her mind. It's as if her motor ran down, and I wish I could find the key to wind her back up again.

She gets her wind back when we reach the end of Bank Street. That's where Wellington Street is and, across it on the other side, Parliament Hill. She stands on the street corner at Bank and Wellington yelling at the Parliament buildings.

"You stupids, you stupids, you stupids!" she yells, cupping her hands and bouncing up and down.

Diablo and I stand a little way off until she quiets down.

"They're so stupid," she says. "They're the ones who should be catching Tronido, not us. Not kids. They don't even care about kids."

"Isn't that a job for the police?"

She rolls her eyes magnificently—the best eye-roller ever. "And who do you think tells the police what to do?"

It never occurred to me that anyone told the police what to do, so I don't say anything. Kathy knows a lot of things I don't.

"I think we *should* try to catch it," I say. "I know it's big and I know it's real, but if we put our heads together, I bet we could do it."

I'm serious and she must see it in my face because she doesn't say anything sarcastic.

"The problem," she says, "is that he isn't around all the time. No one's ever seen him in the daytime and there have only been a few sightings at night."

"Always in the same place?"

"Always."

I give this some serious thought. "What if we all got together and made an expedition in the daytime to see if we can find any clues. Find where he lives."

"We tried that," she says. "We didn't find a thing."

We're standing beside the entrance to the Capitol Theatre. There's a poster of Harry Belafonte. He's coming to Ottawa. I can't believe it. "Well, it's true," she says, and takes a picture of me pointing at the poster. Then we walk on without saying anything, just wandering around in our own thoughts.

I'm thinking how much I like the idea of being inside that little powder-blue plastic box of a camera lying right next to her heart. Until I remember the panther was in there once, too.

A MAN FOR ALL SEASONS

That evening my mother tells me it's my turn to walk Kincho. She is ironing sheets at her sit-down sheet-ironing machine that she got for Christmas.

"Don't you care if I get eaten?"

"It's still light," she says. "Aren't panthers nocturnal feeders?"

I stand there staring at her, hardly able to believe how unworried she is.

All the way to Adams Park I think about catching the panther. I have no idea how, but I know we can do it. James is smart and Sami is smart and Kathy is unbelievably brave, going out like that again and again to photograph it. Surely we can do it.

But as I walk along, I imagine it's just me who catches it, all by myself. There would be a picture in the *Ottawa Journal* and the *Ottawa Citizen* of me standing with my foot on the panther's big black head. Kathy would be so proud of me.

"I'm free to be happy again, thanks to you," she would say.

It may still be light, but night is coming on. All the trees and bushes in the park are rolling out their shadows like the mats we rolled out in kindergarten at nap time. Kincho and I walk the path. We stay in the middle, away from the deep, dark bushes on the north side. We walk all the way to Bank Street and then under it through the little arched tunnel where people have written their names on the curving walls: LA LOVES ER; CF LOVES BV. There are rude words, too, and bad drawings. Someone has drawn a huge mushroom-shaped cloud—the rudest thing of all.

Then we come out into the failing light and there, right in front of me, is Dump Orbit sitting on the wet lawn. His head is bent, his sign lying beside him, a bright yellow rectangle on the grass, the only brightness left in the day. The beatnik is sitting on his heels right next to him.

Kincho barks. His tail is wagging. Only the beatnik looks up.

"SBB," he says. "Alphonse, here, is having himself a bad day." I'm surprised to hear him use Dump Orbit's real name. I feel like I should tell him mine. He's not wearing his shades. I can see that his eyes are light brown tinged with green and gold, like the filbert nuts Mum roasts at Christmas.

I'm just about to introduce myself when Dump Orbit looks up at me and scowls. He picks up his END OF THE WORLD sign and shakes it in my direction.

"Foutus jeunes," he says. *"Pourquoi ne laissez-vous pas un vieux tranquille?"*

Which is when Kincho does this amazing thing. He drags me right over to Dump Orbit and starts licking his face.

"Non," says Dump Orbit, throwing up his arms in defense. I try to drag Kincho off but with no luck. *"Non, non,"* cries the old man, but his voice has changed and next thing I know he's chuckling. "Big stupid dog, eh?" he says.

I kneel beside them, but out of reach in case the old man remembers I'm a kid and kicks me. I can't take my eyes off his face. It's so yellow, like one of my many experiments in Paint by Numbers. He glances at me out of the corner of his eye, but then Kincho licks him again, right in the eye, and he has to cover up with his gnarly old hands.

He's wearing a threadbare brown coat, a filthy gold woolen scarf, and rust-colored fingerless gloves. His gray hair is sticking out as if he stuck his finger in a light socket.

Kincho barks at him. He barks at Kincho.

I look at the beatnik. He's smiling. "Looks like the cavalry arrived in the nick of time," he says. Then he stands up and stretches and his knees crack. "Want a hand, Alphonse?" he asks, but Alphonse wags his head. He and Kincho are wrestling. Alphonse is chatting away in French. It's unbelievable.

"Isn't he hot in that coat?" I ask quietly, although Kincho is making such a racket I doubt the old man can hear me.

"Not as hot as he'll be in an hour or two. That's when he

dresses for winter. He'll be all wrapped up as if the icy winds of December are blowing right in his face. What you see here is his evening attire."

"I don't get it."

Kincho is dragging on Dump Orbit's sleeve as if he wants to take him somewhere. Maybe the dog likes his smell. Dump Orbit scolds him in French and Kincho stops what he's doing right away.

I can't believe it. *Kincho speaks French!*

"It's pretty groovy," says the beatnik. "Each part of the day is a new season for Alphonse. The morning is spring, the afternoon summer, and the evening fall. In the dead of night, ah, well . . . " He pauses. "Every night is winter in his head, as cold as the space he's traveling through on his lonely orbit, the old earth's saddest moon."

Poor, sad Dump Orbit. Except he doesn't look so sad right now. He's having a ball! He tries to get up and then laughs when Kincho knocks him down again.

"Where does he live?" I whisper.

"Alphonse? He's got a niece around here somewhere. She and her family put him up."

"Like that?" I'm trying to imagine my mother letting anyone who smelled so bad into the house.

"They've got a grandfather apartment. A place tacked onto the house. He's an independent kind of guy. Yvette—that's his niece's name—she looks in on him, makes sure he's okay, but otherwise they just let him be." The beatnik looks at his watch. "She'll be here soon to take him home."

I'm glad to hear he has a home. I remember what James said about people taking him away to the funny farm. I'm glad he doesn't have to live there.

"On the weekends they go to the cottage," says the beatnik. "Yvette and her husband and kids. They leave Alphonse here. I don't think he always remembers to go home on those nights."

Just then we both notice a woman walking toward us. She's coming from O'Connor Street in the east, so what's left of the sun lights her up as if she's walking right into a movie. Her face is round like the sun. She places her hand over her eyes as she nears us.

"*Bonjour,*" she says to the beatnik.

"*Bonjour, Yvette,*" says the beatnik. "*Comment vas-tu?*"

"*Je vais bien,*" she says. Then she looks at me and says, "Allo, how are you?"

I just nod because she is so beautiful and French, I can't think straight.

Then she turns to Dump Orbit, who she calls "*Oncle,*" but even I can tell what that means. She pats Kincho on the head before I can warn her that he's dangerous. He sure doesn't look dangerous right now. Then she says, "*Viens-t'en, mon oncle.*"

I'm pretty sure she's telling him it's time to go, but he and Kincho are too busy arguing over who gets to keep a stick. She watches them for a moment and then grins at us.

"What can you do?" she says.

I'm sure Alphonse heard her. He has a look in his eye just like the Sausage when you tell him it's time for his bath. Yvette bends down and strokes the old man's arm. *"As-tu oublié tes compagnons de guerre?"* she says, gently. *"Oncle Alphonse, n'oublie pas les Vandoos."* She pushes the hair back from his face. *"Ils t'attendent. Ils comptent sur toi. Tu n'voudrais pas les abandonner, hein?"*

He lets go of the stick. He's smiling now. *"Non, je ne dois pas les abandonner,"* he grunts. *"Je me souviens."* Then he slowly gets up off the ground and turns to go.

"Je me souviens." It's like magic, the way the words work on him.

The beatnik picks up the old man's sign and hands it to Yvette. She says goodbye and the two of them head across the park toward O'Connor, arm in arm.

I have to grab Kincho's leash quickly. He barks and barks. Yvette turns, laughing, and waves. *"Au revoir,"* she says. She says it to both of us.

"O-ree voir," I call after her, waving.

But Alphonse doesn't look back. It's as if he's under a spell.

"What happened?" I ask.

"Works every time," says the beatnik.

"What did she say?"

"My French isn't so good, but she was talking about his old regiment. The Vandoos. She was reminding him not to forget them. *"N'oublie pas les Vandoos.* Do not forget the Vandoos. And he said something about not letting them down."

"New blee paw lay Vandoos," I say, proud to be speaking French.

"Not bad," says the beatnik.

We watch Yvette and her old *oncle* almost disappear into the shadows of the trees at the end of the park. I expect to see credits roll, like at the end of a movie.

"He fought in the Great War," says the beatnik.

"So did my dad," I say proudly.

"That would be the Second World War, I'm guessing." I nod. "Well, Alphonse fought in the other Great War. The first one that was supposed to be the last one. She reminds him that his comrades are waiting for him. An old soldier never forgets his comrades, even when he's forgotten everything else."

"New blee paw lay Vandoos." I try it again.

The beatnik smiles. "The legendary Royal Twenty-second. In French you'd say *vingt-deux,* but the English called them the Vandoos and it stuck. He was a brave man, Yvette tells me—a hero." I guess I look surprised. "It's true," he says. "But the war kind of unhinged him. War does that."

The beatnik has to go. We say goodbye and I head home through the tunnel where LA loves ER and CF loves BV, but you can't tell anymore because it's too dark. I think about Dump Orbit as a war hero. I think about him becoming unhinged, like an old door flapping in the breeze. I think about how every day is like a year to him. If that's true, then October 23 would be . . . I try to add up the days . . . a long time away. And if he fought in World War I, he must already be a million years old.

Maybe the end of the world wouldn't seem so bad if you were a million years old.

ELEVEN

The next morning, Mum asks me if I did anything about the pollywogs. For a minute I'm not sure what she's talking about. Then I remember. I look out the back-door window, but I can't see the jar of pollywogs from where I'm standing.

And there is something else I can't see either.

"Did someone take Kincho for a walk?"

Mum joins me at the window, drying her hands on a tea towel.

The back garden looks like the no-man's-land you see in pictures of World War I. Dump Orbit might have run across a landscape just like this when he was a Vandoo. There are craters everywhere. There is no grass left, no flowers, no garden furniture, and no Kincho.

I open the door.

"Kincho?"

Nothing. I walk down the steps of the back stoop. Walking through his poop is like walking through a minefield. I stop halfway out and look around. No dog.

Then I see the hole in the fence. He's gone.

I look back at Mum. She's holding her hands to her mouth and staring down in horror at something on the porch. I rush back to her, not even worrying about the minefield of poop. I'm already preparing for the worst: Kincho's carcass covered in flies. Kincho gutted by a panther.

But all I see is my jar. There's no water in it anymore, and no pollywogs or tadpoles or whatever you want to call them. There is just a thick black sludge of deadness in the bottom of the jar. It stinks to high heaven.

◎ ◎ ◎

I go out searching for Kincho. The first place I try is the park, where I run into Kathy and James. They want to come with me but Kathy doesn't have a bike, so we ditch our bikes at the fort and head off on foot. I try to think like a dog and visit the places he might want to visit: the alley behind the butcher on Bank, the pet store with the pretty white poodle in the window. Kathy knows about a woman who keeps a lot of cats, so we rush over there because I told her how much Kincho hates cats.

We're walking up Second Avenue two hours later when

we run into Sami. His uncle has a restaurant. Dogs sometimes hang out at the back door looking for scraps. We check it out. There was a dog there earlier, but it wasn't Kincho. By then we're tired and Sami says we should go back to his place for lunch.

At Sami's we have tall glasses of frosty cold pomegranate juice. I've never even heard of it, but it tastes good. Then we have bread fresh from the oven. It's nothing like my mother's bread. It looks like it's been run over by a truck, but it tastes good and there's this goop you can put on it made with beans. I stick to sliced tomatoes. There's cheese, as well, which is salty and I kind of like it. It sure isn't Kraft slices! For dessert Mrs. Karami serves us something called yogurt. It's made out of dead milk. I make a face when I taste it, which makes Sami and his brother Walli and his little sister Sara laugh. Kathy and James have already tasted yogurt and so they put plenty of honey in theirs. Mrs. Karami sprinkles candied violets on the yogurt so it looks like something you'd eat in a fairy tale.

We sit out in Sami's backyard on lawn chairs in the shade. It's too hot to search anymore.

"Another victim," says Kathy.

I know what she means: Tronido strikes again.

"I've been thinking about what you said yesterday, Rex. You're right. It's time."

Everyone looks at me.

"We've got to catch him," I say. "Tronido, I mean. We can do it."

"Yeah, right," says James.

"I know he's big and strong and he can kill a cow, but we're smart. We could outfox him if we put our minds to it."

Kathy is shaking her head even though she was the one who brought it up. James seems really curious about a tear in the fabric of his chair. Sami is the only one who looks interested. I tell them how the Red Army on their feisty little Siberian ponies outflanked the mighty German war machine.

"But we don't have any ponies," says Kathy.

"Are you saying we should wait until winter?" asks James.

"No," says Sami. "I know what you mean. We just have to be crafty. We have to use our brains."

"And we need weapons," says Kathy.

"Or traps," says James.

"There was a trap in one of the Abbott and Costello movies where they dug a hole, put some meat in it, and then covered it with grass," says Sami. "We could do that."

"Or get a looped rope," I say, "and hang it from the bent branch of a tree and hide it—the rope, I mean—so that when the panther steps into it, it springs up and there's your panther, hanging by its back leg."

"Like in *Peter and the Wolf*?" says Kathy. "Come on, guys! This is real. If we're going to talk about this seriously, we are going to need a serious trap—a real trap."

We all think for a moment. "We have mousetraps at home," says James. "Maybe if we got enough of them?"

He looks as if he's serious, then he starts laughing and we all laugh, even Kathy. We imagine a panther covered in mousetraps. It reminds me of my older sisters with their hair up in rollers.

"Wait a second," says Sami, who jumps up from his chair and races into the garage. There's a lot of noise and he comes back a moment later carrying a lobster trap. "We got it on a holiday in Nova Scotia," he says. "What do you think?"

Now we're all rolling around. Kathy makes us sit up so she can take our picture. Sami looms above us with his mouth open as if he's Godzilla. I bet it's a good picture.

◎ ◎ ◎

That night at home I draw pictures of Kincho and we make posters. I want them to read WANTED, DEAD OR ALIVE, but that makes the Sausage cry. It's not that he ever liked Kincho. He just cries at everything these days.

"Answers to the name of Kincho," writes Letitia, who has the best handwriting.

"Ha!" I say. "He doesn't answer to anything."

I try Kathy's great line at dinner that night. "Another

victim," I say, shaking my head sadly at my plate of steak-and-kidney pie.

"Nonsense," says my mother. "It's perfectly delicious."

◎ ◎ ◎

We keep searching for Kincho the next day, and the one after that. Kathy borrows James's sister's bike. We travel miles and miles. Up to Mooney's Bay and the Hog's Back, which is really just a hill. We ride up to the Le Breton Flats and along the Ottawa River all the way to Island Park Drive. We ride across the river until we're actually in Quebec. *Merci Bon Dieu!*

We take a break on Friday and go swimming at the Shadow: Kathy, James, Sami, Walli, and me. I lend Kathy a quarter without anybody else knowing.

The swimming pool is two basements down, underneath the cafeteria. I float on my back looking up at the gold ceiling, thinking about the chocolate éclairs in their glass compartments just one floor above me, waiting for someone to come and eat them. I know I should be thinking about Kincho and how much I miss him. That's what Timmy would be doing on *Lassie*. People on TV always love their dogs and cry when they run away. But people on TV have beautiful, smart dogs that rescue drowning children and catch bad guys. Kincho just eats lawn chairs and barks at people and pulls my arms out of their sockets when I have to take him for a walk.

Kathy floats up to me on her back just then and asks me what I'm thinking about. I don't want to tell her about Kincho. And I don't want to tell her about the chocolate éclairs, because I don't have enough money to buy one for everybody and it would be hard to split an éclair five ways.

So I say, "I was thinking how this would make a cinchy bomb shelter if you filled the pool with tomato soup."

I look over and she's staring up at the gold ceiling, scowling.

"That is so dumb," she says.

"I know, I was just kidding. Wonder Bread would be a lot better."

"There is no bomb," she says.

I stop floating on my back and tread water. "There isn't?"

She shakes her head violently. "They just made it up to scare kids." And then she rolls over and dives to the bottom of the pool, where she scoots all the way to the deep end without coming up for air.

I wonder if maybe there was something in the newspaper. Maybe the bomb was a big hoax. That would be great and it makes me feel guilty, because before I started thinking about chocolate éclairs and not missing Kincho, I had been having this wonderful daydream. I imagined Kathy and me living in the Shadow after they drop the bomb. The only survivors. We would swim every day and eat chocolate éclairs every night. The pool would be filled with tomato soup, so we would be perfectly safe from nuclear fallout and we would stay in the cafeteria only long enough to grab some éclairs and run.

It was a beautiful dream. Kathy and I floating around for twelve years in tomato soup.

◎ ◎ ◎

And then it's my birthday party.

Dad was going to take the family to the Star Top Drive-in to see *The Comancheros* and *Sniper's Ridge* in a double bill, but he had to go away on business. So instead I'm allowed to invite my new friends to the Mayfair to see *The Road to Hong Kong* and then bring them home for supper. I even manage to convince my mother *not* to make anything English like bangers and mash or steak-and-kidney pie or kedgeree. I show her the newspaper. Hamburger buns are on sale for ten cents a package of eight and ground beef is thirty-nine cents a pound. The best thing is that Top Valu ice cream is only sixty-seven cents a half-gallon.

"It's too good a deal to pass up," I say. And, miraculously, she agrees.

I invite everybody, but James can't come because he's been invited to Buster's grandmother's cottage for the weekend. I know my party will still be fun, but I'm a little jealous. I wonder if I will ever stay in one place long enough to be somebody's best friend. The friend you invite to your grandmother's.

Saturday isn't really my birthday—Sunday is—but we have the party on Saturday because the movie theatres aren't open on Sunday, and anyway, I wouldn't be allowed to go to a party on Sunday, which would be crazy since it's my birthday.

We have a great time. The movie's great and the dinner's great, even though Mum puts out her own condiments along with the Heinz ketchup and French's mustard.

"Branston Pickle?"

"Worcestershire sauce?"

"Pickled walnuts?"

It turns out okay because everybody decides to try out everything and we make a concoction. Flora Bella and I are forbidden to make concoctions, but Mum lets my friends do it. Sami says he really likes the pickled walnuts. For dessert Mum makes an angel food cake and everybody says it is the best cake ever.

All the kids leave around seven, and when they're gone I sit on the front step feeling full and happier than I can remember being in a long time. The Sausage didn't cry and Flora Bella didn't put anything on her nose. She sat watching everyone and listening to everything, and they all said she was a great little sister. My big sisters didn't show up, except for Letitia, which was fine because she said how nice everybody looked and how glad she was to meet them. I was afraid Annie Oakley might decide to shoot somebody, but she wasn't around, and Cassiopeia had locked herself in her room with her new Pat Boone album.

But the very, very best part of the day was that nobody talked about Tronido and nobody talked about bomb shelters. Sami and Walli brought me a model airplane, an F-16; Kathy brought me a slinky. I think it was used but it still had a lot of slinkiness in it. It couldn't have been a better day.

I am eleven. Life is good.

And that's when the cop car pulls up in front of our house.

t's Annie Oakley. She's under arrest. That's all I can find out at first. We all crowd around Mum when she goes to the door to speak to the police officer. She shoos us away and sends Annie to her room. Letitia gets to hang around. The officer wants to question her.

It's so unfair! I sit with Flora Bella at the top of the stairs listening as hard as we can, but we can't hear much of anything.

Finally, the officer drives away. Mum goes up to talk to Annie. Flora Bella and I wait until she closes the bedroom door behind her, and then we crowd together, listening. If life was like a movie we would learn everything, but all we hear is Mum raising her voice and saying, "Wait until your father gets home." Annie doesn't say anything. I peep through the keyhole and see her sitting on her bed straight as a statue while Mum scolds her. Annie's eyes are as black and hard as coal.

Her hands are curled into fists on her powder-blue bedspread.

We scurry away as Mum leaves. As soon as she goes downstairs we find Letitia in her bedroom.

"What happened?" I ask her. "What did the cop want?"

She's writing in her diary. She closes it and presses it to her chest. "Officer Kent?" she says.

"How would I know?"

She sighs. "Wasn't he brawny?"

"What did he say, what did he say?"

Whenever I *have* to talk to Letitia about something important, like the arrest of her younger sister, for instance, I wish I had a torture chamber like in *Shock Theatre*. Letitia's nice, but it would be good to have a rack to stretch her out on when you need to get information fast.

Finally she tells me as much as she knows.

"Officer Kent wanted to know why Annie might have broken into a convent."

"A convent," I say. "Is that where nuns live?"

"A nunnery, yes."

"And?"

"Well, all I could think of was that maybe she's thinking of taking the veil herself, and wanted to see what it was like."

"She took somebody's veil?"

"No, a Bible, I think. Taking the veil is an expression. When you become a nun, you take the veil because you are a bride of Christ."

I can't imagine Annie Oakley wanting to be anybody's bride, let alone Christ's. But the Bible part is interesting. Letitia can't tell me any more. I stamp my foot.

"It's me he should have talked to," I say.

"Officer Kent?" She sighs again. "He was wearing a wedding ring. But maybe his wife died in childbirth and he's only wearing it until someone comes along who can make him forget his sorrow."

I howl and run downstairs and out onto the porch to see if he's still there, sitting in his car writing out his report, like Detective Friday in *Dragnet*. But he's gone.

I could have explained to him what Annie was doing at the convent. *Me.* Not my drippy sister. Talking to a police officer about a case would have been the best birthday present ever. What's the point of being eleven if people still treat you like a kid?

Annie won't talk to anyone. She just stays in her room. And Mum won't listen to me when I try to explain.

"Call Officer Kent," I tell her.

"Oh, yes, please," says Letitia.

But Mum is scandalized. That's what she says. "I will not have the police coming here again. What will the neighbors think?"

Annie's not going to jail or reform school. Her only punishment is that she's not allowed out of the house for the rest of the summer.

I was hoping for handcuffs, at least.

It's late on Sunday when Dad gets home, but I manage to wake up when I hear the car in the driveway. I sneak downstairs just in time to hear Mum telling him what happened.

Dad is sitting in his favorite chair in the living room with his tie off and his waistcoat unbuttoned. He has a little glass of whiskey in his hand.

"She broke into a convent?" he says. "I hadn't pictured our Annie as the religious kind."

"Oh, be serious," Mum says. "She was trying to rob one of the nuns."

"Rob her of what? Her pogo stick? Her stamp collection?"

"Humphrey! This is a very grave matter. They caught her red-handed. She had gone through all the nun's drawers and was sneaking out with a Bible when one of the sisters caught her."

My father almost spits up his whiskey. "A Bible? Annie Oakley?"

Mum places her hand on her heart. "I don't know what was going on in her poor, warped little mind. Oh, Humphrey, what are we to do with her?"

I can't take it anymore. I step out of the shadowy hallway.

"I know what she was doing," I say. It gives Mum a fright

to see me, but Dad seems pleased and asks me to hop up on his lap. I give him a kiss on his bristly home-from-a-trip cheek, but I sit on another chair. After all, I'm eleven now. Then I explain about the nun being a Communist spy.

"Annie was probably looking for a tiny camera or capsules with secret messages in them or a gun. Everybody knows a Bible is a perfect place to hide a gun."

Mum is scandalized all over again. But even though Dad sends me off to bed, I don't think he's scandalized. He tries to look stern, but I can see the smile behind his eyes. He calls to me on the stairs.

"You're quite the detective," he says.

It starts to rain and I can't help thinking about Kincho again. He wasn't much of a pet, but I hate to think of him out in the cold soaking wet.

It rains so much I'm not allowed out on Monday at all. I want to phone James and tell him about my sister getting arrested—well, sort of—but Mum won't even let me use the phone.

Everybody is miserable. Cassiopeia can't afford to buy the fancy new raincoat she wants and she's angry that Mum and Dad won't lend her the money. Letitia is pining over Officer Kent or Clem Keaton or Peter Gunn. Flora Bella is angry because I won't play dolls with her. The Sausage wants Mum to pick him up all the time. *Arrghhh!*

It's as if Annie Oakley, silent as the grave and locked in her room, is an evil black force sucking the life out of the House of Punch.

Tuesday it rains again, just as hard, but today Mum *makes* us go out. I have to take Flora Bella and the Sausage for a walk. I'm not allowed to use Kincho's choke chain either. The Sausage cries because he thinks I'm really going to use it. Flora Bella cries because she really misses the dog.

"Look what you've done now," says Mum, as if it's my fault.

We walk past Buster's house. I want to see if they've got a roof on the bomb shelter yet, but I don't think I'd better sneak up the driveway, not with Flora Bella and the Sausage. I imagine the dug-up garden turning to mud and the mud filling the bomb shelter.

We walk past James's house. I'm hoping he'll look out the window and see us and invite all three of us in and his nice mother will say, "What a darling sister and little brother you have, Rex Zero. Why don't I entertain them while you and James spend the whole afternoon playing?"

We pass by twice. No one sees us.

When we get home, Mum gives us soup with popcorn in it. It's a recipe she got from Mary Moore's Meals. Soggy popcorn. But then, the whole world is soggy.

Mum puts the Sausage down for his nap, and Flora Bella is being so annoying she makes her have a nap, too. Bored with everything, I go down to the basement to look at old *Punch* magazines.

To my surprise, I find the door to the room with the magazines and arrows in it locked. I wiggle the doorknob and push against the door with my shoulder like Mike Hammer in *Kiss Me Deadly* when he's got to find the great whatsit before it blows up the world.

"Go away."

"Is that you, Annie?"

"No. It's Vincent Price, and if you come in I'll turn you into a fly and squash you."

I listen. I hear a thump and then another thump. Then, as if I, Rex Zero, have X-ray vision, I guess what she's doing.

"Are you building a bomb shelter?"

Silence. Then the door opens.

"Shhhh," she says, and pulls me in, locking the door behind her.

In the center of the room is the heavy old mahogany table that must have come from far-off Rangoon. Only, Annie has piled the volumes of *Punch* on the floor all around it like a thick wall. The books go right up to the tabletop. She's used every one.

I crawl behind Annie into the dark little room under the table. Then we sit cross-legged and look around, not saying anything. She's already got some canned food down here. Cabbage rolls, Viennese sausages, ravioli. It's a start.

"Look," she says. And she holds up a bow—a real Indian bow.

"Where did you find it?"

"Behind the bookcase. It must have fallen off the top shelf."

It's real, all right—as real as the arrows in the old quiver. Wow!

She pounds the wall of books with her fist. "It's really solid, try it."

I pound it, too. It doesn't move.

"And the good thing is," I say, "if we get bored, we can read the magazines."

She glares at me and I realize that it wouldn't be safe to take one of the volumes out of the wall and let all the radiation come pouring in.

We sit there in the dark for a minute. Then I lean in close and whisper, "Did you find anything?"

She knows what I'm talking about. She shakes her head. "I would have if I'd had more time."

"In the Bible, right?"

She nods. "I didn't get a chance to look inside, but it felt way too heavy for just a book."

She pounds the musty old carpet, and the thump of her fist brings up a little plume of dust. "They've got to be stopped."

"The Reds?"

"Not just the Reds. The Yanks, too. They blew up an island," she mutters. "Did you know that?" I didn't. "A whole island in the Pacific Ocean somewhere. They used an H-Bomb." The silence in our tiny room inside a room settles like concrete around us.

I suddenly realize something. We are in the House of Punch inside the House of Punch.

◎ ◎ ◎

Annie comes down to dinner that night but only so she can drop her own bomb. "Why would they do that?" she says. "Why would they blow up an island?"

"I know about it," says Letitia, smiling. "They were wearing bikinis when they did it."

"Well, it gets quite hot in the Pacific," says Mum.

Father shakes his head as he cuts a Brussels sprout into quarters. "It was the island of Bikini," he says. "It was just a test. And it happened years ago. Back in the early fifties."

"The whole island disappeared," says Annie. "It was there one moment, and when the dust settled it was gone. There was just water."

"It was a very small island," says Father. "They moved everyone off it. All the animals, too."

"The worms?" asks the Sausage.

"I'm sure the Americans did all they could to make sure no one suffered," says Mum.

"What about the fish?" says Annie. "Did they take all the fish out of the ocean? Where did they move them to?"

The Sausage starts to cry. "Poor fishies," he says between sobs.

"Oh, now look what you've done," says Mum.

"Don't blame me," says Annie Oakley, stabbing her chicken leg as if it's an enemy soldier.

Cassiopeia clears her throat and touches her napkin to her lips. "There's a man at Birks who says that those two new cosmonauts are spying on us. The ones who went up on the weekend."

"Vostok III and Vostok IV!" I shout. I know all about it. It's history's most thrilling chase. That's what it says in the papers. The U.S.S.R. launched two manned satellites into the same orbit 150 miles above the earth. They came so close they could smile and wave to each other. And the best thing is, it was on my birthday.

"It puts the Russians way ahead in the space race," says Dad. "Who knows what they'll do next?"

"It's what they're doing now that worries me," says Cassiopeia. "This fellow at work says they can see right into our houses, even at night. They can see us getting undressed for bed."

"Nonsense," says Father.

"Just remember to keep your curtains shut," says Mum.

"The fellow at work—is he the one with the scrummy eyes you were telling me about?" asks Letitia.

Cassiopeia smiles just a little so as not to upset her makeup. "He's very smart. Mr. Odsburg. Brian. He works in china."

Flora Bella and I frown at each other across the table. "I thought you said he worked at Birks?" I say.

The smile vanishes from Cassiopeia's face. She throws down her silverware. "I cannot stand this family," she says. "I am going to my room and do not wish to be disturbed." Then she leaves but stops at the door and turns back. "If you hear a lot of noise in my room, it's me packing."

We all look at one another with shocked surprise. And then Flora Bella says, "May I have her room, please?" and we all crack up. Even the Sausage. Even Annie.

It's good to see her laughing. I wasn't sure she was ever going to laugh again.

◎ ◎ ◎

That night I lie in bed staring up at my peaked ceiling, thinking of the cosmonauts waving to each other from their satellites. I imagine them streaking by my window waving at me. Their pictures are in the paper. They're smiling. They look nice. They don't look like they want to blow anyone up.

Then I think of the brave Red Army on their Siberian

ponies. There they are with those hats pulled down over their faces against the stinging cold wind. Balaclavas. It's so cold the Nazi tanks are frozen stiff. The famous Panzer Division. The Americans had the Sherman and the Nazis had the Panzer . . .

Panzer? Is that the German word for *panther*?

I fall asleep thinking about that. About me and my brand-new friends surrounding a mighty panther frozen solid. We've all got spears and look scary in our balaclavas.

THE THIEF

Dad has the newspaper all spread out on the kitchen table when I come down for breakfast. There is a picture on the front page of a bunch of kids in gas masks. NEW FACE AT THE FAIR says the headline.

"It's another silly fad," says Dad. "They're selling gas masks for thirty-five cents but they're not worth a plug nickel."

"What fair do they mean?" I ask.

"The Ex," says Letitia. "It's the big end-of-summer fair. There are rides and cotton candy and Kewpie dolls a boy can win for his girl."

"Can we go?"

"We'll see," says Mum, but it doesn't sound promising. She's looking at those kids in their gas masks as if she doesn't like what she sees.

It's still a bit rainy but I go out anyway. I see one of our posters for Kincho taped to the streetlight at the corner of

Lyon and Clemow. The ink has run, so you can't tell what's being looked for or where to phone if you find it. I tear it down, roll it into a ball, and throw it in the first trash can I find.

Kathy is in the tree house huddled in a blanket. Her eyes look frightened when I poke my head through the trapdoor, but then they light up, as if she's glad to see me.

"Are you okay?" I ask.

"That man—the old crazy kook with the sign—he yelled at me," she says.

I sit beside her. "He yells at everybody. I saw him yelling at a squirrel once."

"That isn't all. He grabbed at me."

I'm shocked. I can't imagine Dump Orbit as a pervert. "What do you mean?"

"He grabbed at me, Rex. He was swearing in French and just making swipes at me. I jumped away but he kept coming." She wrinkles her nose. "He stinks."

I tell her about how he was a soldier in the First World War. "He's a little crazy," I explain.

"I'd say a *lot* crazy." She sniffs, but she doesn't say any more. She shivers. The floor is wet. I wonder how long she's been here.

"Are you cold?" I ask.

"No," she says. She's really shivering and her eyes look sad and kind of lost.

Suddenly I have a great idea. "I've got the perfect thing."

I scramble to my feet and start to shimmy down the ladder. "I'll be right back," I say, like a real hero, like someone who knows exactly what to do in a pinch.

I race home. Diablo has never galloped faster. In the house, Mum is upstairs Hoovering—I mean vacuuming. Good. I run to the pantry where we keep the canned food just in case the Battle of Britain breaks out. I find a can of tomato soup, open it, and pour it into a saucepan and heat it on the stove.

At one point the Sausage walks in with one of his teddy bears dressed in a diaper. "He's wetting his bed a lot," says the Sausage. "Because of the war coming."

I fill a thermos bottle with the heated soup and don't spill a drop. In no time I'm back at the tree house.

Kathy is still there, wrapped in her blanket looking miserable. I pour her a cupful of steaming tomato soup. She looks at me as if it's a trick.

"It's good," I say confidently. I am Dr. Kildare. I never lose a patient.

Her hand worms out from under the damp blanket and she takes the plastic mug. She sips and her eyes close. Now her other hand appears and she holds the mug with both hands.

"He wanted my camera," she says.

It takes me a minute to remember what she's talking about. "Dump Orbit?"

She takes another sip of soup. "I took his picture by the

fountain and he got really mad. That's when he started yelling at me. It was really scary."

Just then, it starts to rain again. We huddle near the trunk of the tree but it's coming at us sideways.

"My place," I shout into her ear, so she can hear me above the raindrops exploding like a million tiny bombs on the platform of the fort. She nods and we run for it.

When we get there Mum says she ought to throw us in the dryer for a spin or two. Kathy looks a little scared, especially when Flora Bella suggests we throw her down the laundry chute first. But then the Sausage wanders into the kitchen and hands Kathy his second-best teddy.

Mum sends me off to my room to change, and when I come down Kathy is sitting in the kitchen in a huge pink quilted robe that used to belong to Letitia or Cassiopeia.

For lunch we have Tennessee Ernie Ford's favorite beans-and-hamburger dish, which Mum found in a magazine, and fresh baked bread. Kathy doesn't have a TV. She's never seen Tennessee Ernie Ford, but she's amazed by the bread and eats about a hundred slices. I'm kind of proud.

Then Flora Bella appears in her polka-dot dress. She introduces Kathy to the polka dots: Miranda, Cassandra, Doranda, Veranda . . . until Mum makes her stop. Kathy's clothes are dry by then. When she comes back downstairs after changing, her hair is neatly brushed and pulled back in a ponytail, the way it was the first time I saw her.

While she was upstairs, I cleaned off her Brownie with a

tea towel. I think of all of us in that camera, together. Me outside the theatre, Sami and James and me in Sami's backyard, and now Dump Orbit. I hope we're all getting along okay.

It's still pouring when the Sausage and Flora Bella go for their nap, so I take Kathy downstairs to see Annie Oakley's bomb shelter. I don't know where Annie is. She must be up in her room since she's not allowed out. We sit inside the bomb shelter for a while, but the only thing that interests Kathy is the bow and arrows.

She inspects the old arrows in the dim light under the table, holding each of them close to her eye like a blind person, feeling the sharpness of the flint arrowheads.

We go upstairs after a while and break out the Ouija board. She has never seen one before.

"My sisters use this to figure out who is going to marry them," I tell her. She screws up her face. "It can foretell your future," I say in a quavery, mysterious voice. She just shakes her head and walks over to the window. Thunder booms from a long way off. I count: one steamboat, two steamboats, three steamboats . . .

"It's fourteen miles away," I say in my best expert voice. Kathy is kneeling on the window seat looking out at the street. The downpour has stopped, but the wind is shaking the rain out of the trees so it's still pretty wet.

"I left my sweater in the bomb shelter," she says all of a

sudden, and then heads down the hall to the basement stairs.

I set up the Ouija board. I even go upstairs and get a towel to wrap around my head like a real swami. I borrow a broach from Cassiopeia's room to hold the turban together. I sit cross-legged on the living room carpet, my back straight, my arms folded across my chest, the Ouija board in front of me, waiting.

Waiting.

Waiting.

It takes me a long time to realize she's gone. I check the bomb shelter. Gone. I ask the Ouija board if Kathy hates me. It spells out *no*.

Well, that's something anyway.

That evening I'm in my room thinking about working on a new Paint by Numbers, when I hear a wild shrieking from downstairs, as if someone is pouring burning hot oil all over themselves.

It's Annie Oakley. Someone stole her bow and arrows.

A PLAN

I have to get the bow and arrows back right away and it's not just because Annie Oakley is going to kill me. Mum and Dad look like they want to kill me, too.

"It's a dangerous weapon," says Mum.

"It's a valuable artifact," says Dad.

"It's mine!" says Annie, and Dad has to hold her back from beating me to a pulp.

"It is not yours!" I yell back at her.

"It does not belong to either of you," says Dad, burying Annie in a big hug. "It belongs to the owner of this house. And it is not a toy. Do you understand, Rex?"

I nod. "I'll get it back. I'm sorry."

"What can that young lady have been thinking?"

"She's afraid," I say.

"Afraid? Dear me. Of what?"

I don't get adults. You have to beat them over the head before they understand anything.

"They're all afraid of the big black panther who lives in the park," says Annie.

My parents look at her in astonishment and then at me.

"Is it true, Rex? Is there really a panther?"

"Of course not," says Annie. And then she stomps up to her room.

I yell up the stairs at her, "There is, too! There is, too! I saw it and you didn't."

But then I'm dragged off to the kitchen so that I don't wake anyone up. Mum makes me sit and have some hot milk to calm me down and help me sleep. Cassiopeia comes into the kitchen and, when she sees me, glances meaningfully at her watch.

"Shouldn't you be in bed?" she says.

"I thought you were moving out."

"And miss all the fun?"

◎ ◎ ◎

I lie in bed thinking. Thinking of Kathy sneaking through Adams Park—maybe right now—hunting down Tronido. I want to go and stop her, but I'm too frightened without Kincho. He wasn't much of a pet, but he was a great bodyguard.

Somehow I fall asleep and dream of panthers and Panzers, of bow-hunting girls who turn into Red Army soldiers riding Siberian ponies. Then, somehow, those brave Russians turn into brave French Canadian soldiers. Vandoos.

"New blee paw lay Vandoos." And now in my dream it's Dump Orbit Kathy is chasing on horseback, and he is running like crazy toward the Bank Street underpass. Kathy is gaining on him, her legs gripping the sides of her pony. "No one tries to take my Brownie Starflash!" she shouts. She pulls back the bowstring.

"Don't!" I yell at her. "He's not the one you want!"

But she won't stop and she lets the arrow go—

Fwwwwwwt!

I awake with a terrible jerk, as if the arrow she let fly got me in the neck. I lie there barely knowing where I am. My heart is beating so loudly it sounds as if there is someone else in the room with me. I try to stop breathing so that I can hear better. I'm too afraid to turn on my bedside lamp, too afraid to move a muscle.

I stare at my open window, a lighter shade of darkness. The curtains stir. I hear dripping eaves and the *crick crack* of branches rubbing against the roof.

There is something in here that wasn't here before. And then, as my heart calms down a bit, I realize what it is.

It is an idea.

An idea has crept out of the dark cave of my dreams and is cowering somewhere in the room, waiting for me to notice it. As my eyes adjust to the light I can see what a large idea it is. Funny how I couldn't see it before.

I cradle my head in my arms, half afraid the idea will slip away, back into the night. But it stays. I hold on to it. It stays and grows. It curls up with me when I fall asleep again. And when I wake up in the morning it isn't an idea anymore. Like a caterpillar it has transformed.

Now it's a plan.

◎ ◎ ◎

At breakfast, Mum doesn't mention the row we had last night. That's what English people call it, a row. Here it would be called a fight. I am very polite to everyone, even Cassiopeia.

"That's a particularly nice dress you're wearing," I say. She smiles at me. I think of saying that I hope Mr. Odsburg will like it, but decide that might get me into deep water.

I help the Sausage with his breakfast and clean my cereal bowl and his in the sink. Finally, when Mum's busy with something at the counter, I tiptoe down the front hall, out the door, down the steps, and around the side of the house to where Diablo is waiting.

We head straight to the fort. No one is there, but that's okay because I only want to check something in the scrapbook.

Just as I suspected!

My next stop is James's house. I ride fast but carefully, with both hands on the handlebars. The roads are wet and I am carrying valuable cargo. A new plan is like a jar full of pollywogs. I don't want any of them to slop out.

When I get to James's house, Buster is there, home from his grandmother's cottage. They tell me about their weekend: about a tippy canoe and cannonballing off the dock and campfires and marshmallows charred to a crisp. Buster water-skied for the first time—the first time he could actually stay up.

Finally, they ask me what I've been up to and I tell them.

"We're going to capture Tronido?"

I nod. "I've worked it all out."

"Worked it all out—how?"

"I'll tell you later. When we see Kathy. She has to be there. All the panther people have to be there."

Buster looks disappointed. I tell them about Kathy coming over and stealing the bow and arrows.

"I bet she already bagged Tronido last night," says James.

"I don't think so. Not last night."

They look at me in a funny way.

"I'll explain later," I tell them. "But if I'm right, we have to capture him tonight or tomorrow."

James looks very grownup as he thinks this over. Then he sticks out his hand to shake on it. "I'm in," he says. He turns to Buster. "Can you sneak out?"

"I don't know," he says, squirming a bit. "Dad will kill me." He looks excited—excited and scared.

We bike to Kathy's. She lives in a second-floor apartment that you reach by a steep metal staircase that leads up from a neat little courtyard down an alley off Gladstone. Hanging from the iron balcony are flower boxes filled with yellow flowers. Her door is periwinkle blue.

Kathy meets us at the door. She looks happy to see James and Buster, but not so happy to see me. She looks down at her bare feet. Then she turns back into the apartment and comes back with the bow and the arrows.

"Sorry," she says, without looking at me.

"Jumpin' Jehoshaphat," says Buster. "Can I look at that?" He takes the bow from her, and James takes the quiver full of arrows.

"It looks like you tried it out," I say. "Any luck?"

She shakes her head. "I just practiced on a tree."

"You didn't see Tronido?"

She shakes her head. This is a good sign. It means my idea might be right.

"I'm glad you're okay," I say.

Finally she dares to glance at me. I put on a smile. She puts on one, too.

"It was really bad of me," she says. "Especially after your mom made that nice lunch. I just . . . I just thought . . ."

"It's okay."

"Is this how we're going to capture Tronido?" Buster asks, pulling the string on the bow.

"We won't need it," I say. "Believe me. We won't need any weapons. I've got this all figured out."

Kathy looks worried. "What's going on?" she says.

"We're going to catch Tronido tonight," says James. "For once and for all."

Kathy finally invites us all in. Her apartment is small but nice. One wall of the little sitting room is taken up with a kind of shrine to her father. He was a pilot in the Korean War. There are several framed pictures of him looking handsome in his uniform. There's a bunch of medals for bravery. Kathy shows them to us one by one. She is so proud, I'm jealous. Except I'm glad my father is still alive, so I feel guilty for being glad and guilty for feeling jealous.

Finally, we sit down and I tell them the plan, as much as I can. "I'm pretty sure Tronido will be there tonight," I say.

"He wasn't there last night," says Kathy.

"I know. But I'm pretty sure he'll be there tonight. Tonight or tomorrow."

"How are we going to do it?"

I take a deep breath. This is the tricky part. "I can't tell you until tonight. You need to trust me on this."

Kathy is staring at me like a teacher who is hoping you have the right answer when she knows you are the kind of kid who never gets the right answer.

Buster looks scowly now. "You said you were going to tell us," he says.

"When all the panther people are together," I answer.

Buster is not pleased. "I'm getting a bad feeling about

148

this. Are you sure you don't have a secret weapon or some-thing?"

Kathy has this businesslike look on her face. She fishes out a penknife from her pocket. It's a good one. "I never go anywhere without this," she says.

Buster looks a little more hopeful. "I could bring my Louisville Slugger," he says.

"Uh . . . nobody should bring any weapons," I say, a little panicky. "You won't need them. In fact, it might be danger-ous if you bring something."

Three sets of eyes drill a hole into my face.

The plan is so clear inside my head, but if I try to take it out now I'm sure I'm going to slop those poor little squirmy pollywogs all over the place.

I look at Kathy. "You go to the park to photograph Tro-nido all the time."

"Yeah, but I've got my knife."

"Well, then, bring your knife. But let's not bring any other stuff. If he didn't attack you, then he's not going to at-tack if there's a bunch of us there, right?"

"I still have a bad feeling," says Buster.

I look at him and try not to let the fear in his eyes get to me. "I know that you don't know me very well. Maybe I'm the kind of guy who says he can do stuff just to get people's at-tention. But I swear my most excellent swear that I'm not do-ing that. It's going to be safe. I promise."

Buster looks pale.

"Well, I'm going there tonight," I say. "To Adams Park. I'm going to catch Tronido. I think it would be good if we were *all* there, but I don't want you to come if you don't want to."

It gets very quiet in the little room. All you can hear is the traffic out on Gladstone. Then Kathy says, "I believe you."

"If Kathy's going, then I'll go, too," says James.

There's only Buster left. He looks glum. He gazes around the room at the three of us and says, very quietly, "I really, really don't want to do this." Then he stands up and heads for the door.

Kathy jumps up and follows him outside. We can hear them talking a bit, but not very well.

James is tugging on his little silver dollar of gray hair. "You want us to trust you. Why won't you trust me?"

I do trust James. And more than anything in the world I want him to trust me. I haven't had many friends—not ones I got to keep. He might believe my idea, but he might not—and I don't want to risk it.

Luckily, Kathy comes back in then. But without Buster. We hear him clumping down the steel stairs.

"What happened?"

She sits down and curls her feet up under her. "I told him he was brave. It's something my daddy said to me in a letter. I was only a baby when he died, but he wrote me these long letters in case he didn't get to see me. There was this one time he was in a hospital in Korea somewhere. One of the things he said is that I should never do anything that seems dumb just because everybody else is doing it. He didn't say it exactly like that. But he did say this: 'A really brave girl listens to her heart.' "

We sit in silence. I can't believe her father actually wrote that. It sounds good enough to be in *Reader's Digest*. I look at her closely. There is this defiant look in her eye. I think her eyes are saying to me that she trusts in her heart that I am right.

I look at James. I expect to see the serious James Stewart look on his face, like in *The Man Who Shot Liberty Valance*, but instead he's grinning, like James Stewart in *Harvey*, who has this imaginary friend who's a rabbit. I think he's saying that he trusts me, too.

Oh, boy. I hope I'm right.

TRONTDO

Remember when I said how our life is sort of like a board game but I never get to roll the dice? Well, I'm the one rolling the dice now and I'm not so sure I like it. All those times we moved because my dad had a new job, it must have been hard for him. I never thought of that before. All those people whose lives were being changed—me and my sisters and little brother and Mum. Is this how he felt?

I'm going to have to sneak out of the house, which is not easy when there are five people older than you wandering around like gestapo guards in a prisoner-of-war camp. I have a plan, though. That's the thing about plans. Once you've got one, a lot of others seem to come along.

I need a black shirt, a black hat, and a stout rope. In the *Eagle Annual*, they always have stout ropes. They're the only kind of ropes you can depend on when the going gets tough. I decide to use the one that holds up the tire swing in the backyard, which means I have to climb the tree to untie it.

Dad put it up and the knot is hard to undo, but I manage it with the help of a rat-tail file I find on the workbench in the garage.

I lie for a minute in the branch overlooking the garden. Somebody cleaned up all the wrecked garden furniture. Somebody cleaned up all the poop. The grass is beginning to grow again. Soon you won't even know Kincho was ever here. I'm sad at first and then not sad. I hope he didn't get eaten by anything or run over. But I'm kind of glad he's gone. From here I can see my mother in the kitchen window. I can see the yappy little dog with the squished-in face in our neighbors' backyard.

Then a shiver runs down my back. I have a panther's-eye view of the world.

The black hat is easy: my grandfather's trilby. It's a soft felt hat with a dimple in the top. I don't remember my grandfather, but he must have had a very small head because his trilby fits perfectly. It smells of pipe smoke, like my dad.

The black shirt isn't so easy. But after scouting around I decide on one I find in Cassiopeia's room. It's sort of filmy with puffy sleeves and little black buttons that look like pearls. When I look at myself in the mirror I see a pirate—a pirate in blue jeans with turned-up red cuffs and black Keds.

Here is the escape plan. My bedtime is supposed to be nine-thirty. My mother wants me to get used to going to bed earlier because school is just around the corner. So off I'll go to bed at nine-thirty. I'll complain a bit, or they'll get suspicious. Once I'm tucked in, my parents never check on me until they go to bed after the news and a sandwich and tea at eleven-thirty. I'm hardly ever awake, but I know Mum checks us all the same, even my grownup sisters. Maybe after all the moving we've done, she just wants to make sure she didn't leave one of us behind.

I'm going to escape from the house by climbing down the laundry chute to the basement. That's what the stout rope is for. There's a door from the basement to the outside. I don't think I'm strong enough to climb back up the chute so I have thought ahead and planted a pair of pajamas in the basement. When I get back, I'll slip into my pajamas and try to sneak back up to my room. If my parents catch me I can say I was just getting a drink of water.

"That's funny," they'll say. "We didn't see you come down." And I'll say, "I guess it must have been a really good episode of *Gunsmoke*." Or, if it's later, I'll say, "I guess the news must have been really interesting."

As night comes on, I look out my window and pray to all the cosmonauts in the great big sky that my plan will work.

I make it down the first stage of the laundry chute okay. I put six pillows in the basket at the bottom, just in case. It's hot in here and the filmy black blouse itches. How do girls stand wearing things like this? The good thing is I hardly need the rope at all because the walls are tight around me. I press my back against one wall and my knees against the opposite wall and kind of crawl down.

Everything is going fine. Then, just as I pass by the second floor, I hear Letitia's voice in the hallway nearby. Then the door to the chute opens above me and light spills in and I'm sure she'll see me, but she's too busy talking to Annie Oakley and just throws some stuff in without looking. The door clangs shut and I'm in the dark again, almost suffocating under the laundry on my head. I have to climb the rest of the way covered with slips and bras and panties.

I don't take Diablo. I don't want to use my headlight and I don't like the idea of riding in the dark without it. As I walk up Clemow I see the white car again. The Citroën, looking like an old friend.

It's a chilly night. Fall is moving in. There is no one around. As I turn onto Lyon, a car comes toward me from the north. I hide behind a tree. I am a British agent in Berlin with a secret that will end the war. The car swishes past through the puddles left over from so many days of rain.

I head down Lyon again. I see the lamp that lights up the landing of the stairs down to the park, and someone is waiting. I push my trilby down hard on my ears and stride forward.

It's James. He's wearing a black Ottawa Rough Riders long-sleeved T-shirt with a red number 11 on it. Dave Thelen's number. James's hair is dark enough that he doesn't need a hat, but his little gray spot shines like a splash of moon juice. His eyes shine, too. He's got a hammer tucked into his belt.

"I know you said we wouldn't need any weapons, but I brought one anyway," he whispers.

Kathy arrives next, in a black turtleneck sweater, a black knit hat, and black gloves. She looks like a real cat burglar.

It's time to go, but James looks at his watch and says we should wait another couple of minutes. Sure enough, Sami and Walli arrive.

"I figured we might need backup," says James.

Sami has brought a flashlight. I can't believe I didn't think to bring a flashlight. In the *Eagle Annual*, they *always* have flashlights, except they're called torches. Walli has one, too. He's also got a whip. "It's a genuine Zorro whip," he whispers. Sami has a pocketknife that's even bigger than Kathy's.

"We won't need any weapons," I tell them. I look at James. He shrugs.

"It can't hurt," says Walli.

We start down the stairs and I feel a little better, surrounded by friends.

"Hey."

There's a voice behind us. We look back. Standing under the lamplight at the top of the stairs is Buster. He looks huge, like a superhero, or at least his shadow does. It's already zigzagging its way down the stairs. Soon enough he's with us, out of breath and red in the face. We all clap him on the back.

"My parents went out and the babysitter fell asleep," he says in a whisper.

Then Sami notices what Buster's wearing. "Whoa!" he says. "What's that?"

Strapped to Buster's belt is a sheath, and from it Buster pulls the biggest knife I've ever seen. It has a bone handle and at least a six-inch blade.

"My dad's Bowie knife," he says proudly. In the flashlight glow it looks truly deadly. It frightens me.

"Listen," I say in a loud whisper. "Nobody makes a move until I say so. Okay?"

Everybody nods solemnly, but Buster looks disappointed.

"Put that thing away," I tell him. "I mean it."

Surprisingly, he does as he's told.

The wind picks up and it has a real nip in it. The dense shrubbery moves around as if there is a panther in every tree jumping from branch to branch.

"What was that?" says James, turning suddenly and looking back toward the steps. We all spin around. "I heard something," he whispers. I don't doubt him. James doesn't fool around.

But I don't see a thing. Nobody else does either. After another wait, we turn back toward our goal, a little more nervous than we were a minute before. Surrounded on the north and south by high green living walls painted black by the night and washed by only a trace of moonlight.

I feel like a gladiator walking out into the Coliseum. Actually, I feel more like one of the Christians the Romans liked to throw to hungry lions.

"How are we going to do this?" says Kathy.

"We'll head over to where you and I saw him that other time," I whisper.

"And then what?" says Sami.

"One step at a time," I say.

"We're going to catch the panther?" says Sami.

I nod. "We are."

There is a long silence filled only with wind and stealth and the number 2 bus stopping on Bank Street in another world. I glance at James, but James is looking at Kathy and Kathy is looking at me. She's chewing on her lower lip. I want to say, "You take over. I just moved here. It's your panther." She takes a deep breath and turns to face the enemy. We fall in behind her. She's got her penknife out.

We stop twenty feet from the wall of trees. The darkness looms before us. We listen, trying to hear a deeper rustling than the wind. Kathy turns to me.

What now? I step forward, then I march ahead of the others until I'm only ten feet from the unknown.

"Tronido," I call out, but the sound of my voice isn't very loud. I clear my throat and try again. "Tronido? We know you're in there."

I look back toward the others. None of them has moved. I turn back toward the woods and call again. "Do you hear me? We're here to see you. Come out. Now! We don't want to be scared anymore."

I hear something. The others do, too, because one of them gasps. I hear it again, a rustling in the trees that isn't the wind, because the wind has taken off. Maybe it knows something we don't. The rustling grows louder as it gets closer and then I hear a low growling.

I step back. Somebody whimpers. It might be me.

Then, suddenly, Kathy is beside me, yelling at the darkness. "Get out of here! Get out of here or we'll kill you! Get out! Get out!"

The anger in her voice frightens me as much as the knife in her hand. I reach out to hold her back. Then there is a rumbling growl followed by a snapping and a crashing sound and then the panther is there, bursting out of the bushes, a deeper darkness than the trees, low to the ground, the shape of its head lost between hunched shoulders.

Its black pelt glimmers in the faint moonlight. Its eyes glitter in its black face.

I can't move. I'm frozen with fear.

I was wrong. My whole crazy plan was wrong. The panther growls again and rakes the air with one black paw. He rakes the air with his other paw, too. He's crouching on his hind feet, ready to leap.

He growls and suddenly I know that growl.

It's now or never.

Kathy has grabbed my arm, but I shake her off and step toward the creature. Closer, closer, until I'm only one good leap away.

"New blee paw lay Vandoos," I cry. "New blee paw."

The creature falls to all fours as if he's been shot.

"New blee paw," I shout, taking another step forward. "Lay Vandoos." The creature rears up and growls ferociously, but I am not fooled anymore.

"Monsieur Alphonse?"

"Look out!" cries James. I'm just about to turn to tell him not to worry when I catch a movement out of the corner of my left eye. Something—someone—is running along the edge of the bush, almost invisible, bearing down on the creature in front of us.

Too late, I see the bow, see that it is drawn.

"No, Annie!" I cry. But it is too late. Too late. I hear the *thwang* the arrow makes. Then I hear the sharp cry of pain from the creature, who crumples to the ground. The next thing I know, the others surge past me toward the victim.

"Stop!" I cry, my voice full of rage and fear. "It's not what you think!"

THE OLD SOLDIER

I stand rooted to the spot, feeling the world come crashing down all around me. Everything has gone wrong. It is as if the idea I was carrying around in my head has exploded into a million shards of glass. The wounded figure of an old soldier is rolling on the ground, the gang closing in around him, shouting and cursing. Kathy's knife is raised. Buster is pulling his giant Bowie knife from its sheath. Sami and Walli have their flashlights trained on the thing that I know is Dump Orbit, but they still believe is Tronido.

Then I see Annie drawing back her bow again with a fresh arrow.

"No!" I shout. "Leave him alone!"

I'm not sure anyone hears me, but everyone hears the dog. It comes crashing out of the bushes, as black as a demon, barking like mad and growling ferociously. The beam of a flashlight gleams on its yellow teeth.

Kincho.

Everyone shouts and backs off. Kincho stands, four-square, beside the creature writhing on the ground and bares his teeth in a blood-curdling growl. The others are all crowded around me—all except for Annie. I push my way through the crowd. I grab Sami's flashlight and shine it in my own face.

"It's me, Kincho," I say. "Good dog."

He growls low in his throat, but I take another step forward anyway. I've got to get to Alphonse. The arrow is sticking out of his shoulder and he is moaning in pain. I swing the flashlight around to Annie. I'm not sure if it's the moan or the sudden glare in her eyes, but she looks as if she's woken up from a nightmare. She lowers her bow and I flash the light back to Alphonse, who struggles up and presses a gloved hand to his injured shoulder. Annie gasps. She covers her mouth. Then, before I can stop her, she turns and runs.

"Annie, come back!" I call, but she disappears into the darkness.

"Owww!" cries Alphonse, tentatively feeling the shaft of the arrow, but he sounds more angry than hurt. *"Foutus jeunes. Pourquoi ne laissez-vous pas un vieux tranquille?"*

Then James is at my shoulder. "It's the end-of-the-world man," he whispers.

"Yes."

"You knew?"

"Yes."

"You should have told us."

"I know."

Kincho finally turns his attention away from us and back to Alphonse. He starts to whimper and tries to lick Alphonse's face. I move in and fall to my knees. I pat Kincho. "Good dog." And then I help the old man remove the mask from his face. The balaclava.

The arrow is sticking out from his shoulder, drooping. I grab hold of the shaft carefully and pull and it comes right out. Luckily he's wearing a really thick coat.

"Are you all right?"

The question seems to bring him around. He feels his shoulder where I pulled out the arrow.

"Bon Dieu," he says, "que ça fait mal!"

"It's really hurting him," says Sami.

Alphonse starts to undo his coat—because that is what it is: a huge, mangy old winter coat made of pelts from a whole lot of black creatures. I try to help him with the buttons, but he slaps me away. He's still wearing gloves—black as well. Leather, but old and cracked.

Meanwhile, Kincho is licking his face and Alphonse has to fight both of us off. James joins us and together we manage to undo the coat and pull it back from Alphonse's wounded shoulder.

Sami steps forward, aiming his flashlight down at the wound. There is blood.

"Bon Dieu," says Sami. "Désolés, monsieur."

Alphonse squints up into the glare of Sami's flashlight

and growls. Then he looks around at us as if he has just finally taken us all in. His eyes land on Kathy. *"Pourquoi voulez-vous bien prendre ma photo?"* he barks. *"Ne pouvez-vous pas laisser un vieux soldat tranquille?"*

I look at Kathy. I don't know what he said and I don't think she knows either. She looks as dazed as he does.

"He asked her why she took his photograph," says Sami. "He says he's just an old soldier. Why can't we just leave him alone?"

"He *is* an old soldier," I say. "A Vandoo, right?"

Now Alphonse looks at me quizzically and nods his head. Then a pained expression spreads over his old face and he squeezes his arm tenderly.

"We'd better get him to a doctor," says James.

"Non!" says Alphonse. "No doctor." He pushes the dog away and takes off his gloves.

"Why would he do this?" says Kathy. "Why would he dress up just to scare us?" She's talking to me, but she's looking at him.

"That isn't why he does it," I tell her. "He thinks it's winter every night. These are his winter clothes, that's all. I don't think he meant to scare anyone."

Kathy shakes her head angrily. "Then why does he growl? Why does he act like he's going to attack?"

"He's not well," I tell her. "He was in World War I and he went kind of crazy."

I put my arm around her shoulder. She shakes me off.

"I think he's afraid of us," I say.

Kathy glares at me. And in her eyes I see her own fear swirling around inside her fury.

"He's not right in the head," I whisper.

And she starts to cry.

"It doesn't look too bad," says James. He's pulled out another of his monogrammed handkerchiefs and dabbed away the blood from the old man's shoulder. Alphonse is sitting quietly and watching, too exhausted to fight anymore. His other arm is draped around Kincho's shoulder. The old man murmurs in the dog's ear, something in French. Kincho looks perfectly pleased with himself.

We all crowd around. It looks as if the arrow only barely pierced Alphonse's skin. There is a tiny puncture in his upper arm—nothing more. Now Walli brings his flashlight closer, too. There is a tattoo lower down on the withered old arm, an amazing tattoo. It's a beaver with a huge crown on its back. There's a coat of arms on the beaver's side and a banner under it that says, *"Je me souviens."* The tattoo is beautiful: red, green, blue, and gold.

"Juma sue veens," I read.

"Je me souviens," says Sami. "It means 'I remember.' "

"That's the Vandoos' slogan," I say. "The Vandoos, yes?" I ask Alphonse.

"Oui," he says.

Sami helps him with his coat. *"Nous ne savions pas que vous étiez soldat."*

"*Nous pensions que vous étiez une panthère,*" says Walli.

"You speak French," I say.

Sami smiles up at me. "We spoke French in Lebanon," he says.

Alphonse clambers to his feet, refusing the offer of any help. We all step back. He looks straight at Sami and jabs his finger at him. "*Vous direz à vos amis de me ficher la paix,*" he says. "*Vous devriez être chez vous au lit. Pas en train de tabasser un vieillard.*"

"*Oui, monsieur,*" says Sami politely. "*Pardon.*"

"What did he say?"

"That we should leave him alone. That we should be at home in bed, not out beating up an old man."

THE END OF THE WORLD, AGAIN . . .

We sit on the stairs by the Lyon Street exit: James, Kathy, Buster, Sami, Walli, and me. Everyone wants to know how I figured out the mystery. So I tell them about Yvette and her family and how she looks after Alphonse except on the weekends, when they go up to their cottage. Then I tell them that when I checked the scrapbook at the fort all the dates of sightings were on weekends.

And then I tell them how I've seen him in all three seasons of his daily clothing, but not winter, so I had to kind of guess about that. And I tell them about the Red Army soldiers at Petrograd and their balaclavas and about the magic words "New blee paw lay Vandoos."

"No wonder it didn't work so well," says Sami. *"N'oublie pas les Vandoos,"* he says. And we all laugh at my French.

When I finally get home it's just after eleven. I go to put the arrow back into the little House of Punch, and run into Annie. She's in her pajamas with the bow across her lap.

She looks up at me, her forehead all bunched with concern.

"He's okay," I tell her. "His coat was pretty thick."

The worry melts away. Now she just looks irritated.

"He's cuckoo," I tell her. "He got injured in the war."

She looks past me at nothing. Then a smile sneaks into the corner of her eye. A wicked smile. "I told you there was no panther," she says.

She's brought pillows and blankets down to the House of Punch. "There are no imaginary things to worry about," she says. "Just the bomb. I'm sleeping here. Don't want to get caught unawares."

She says she saw me when Letitia opened the laundry chute. That's how she knew I was sneaking out. She had a pretty good idea of what I was up to.

"I thought you didn't believe in the panther."

"I didn't. I thought it was a spy."

"Or a mutant?"

"Right. I was worried about you."

I'm not sure what to say, at first. Then it comes to me. "Well, thanks."

She shrugs and looks away. "Are you going to tell?"

I shake my head.

She smiles. And it reminds me of the cosmonauts in

Vostok III and Vostok IV smiling and waving to each other from their separate Sputniks. It's a smile that comes from miles away.

"Tell the old man I'm sorry," she says.

I change into my pajamas and sneak up to the kitchen. I fill a glass of water and head upstairs to bed. As I pass the TV room, Mum hears me.

"Well, well, well," she says.

"I was just getting a drink of water," I say.

"That's funny, we didn't hear you come down."

I nod. "I guess it must have been a pretty good episode of *Gunsmoke*." But when I look at the TV there is some kind of special news bulletin.

"What's that?" I ask.

Dad points his pipe at the television. "The Yanks are getting very jittery about Cuba."

"Oh," I say and head up to my room and my bed under the sloping walls. I'm too tired now for any more wars.

◎ ◎ ◎

I go to the park around sundown on Monday and time it just right, because there is Yvette come to take her old uncle home. Kincho is with him. He barks at me and wags his tail. Alphonse barks and wags his tail, too.

"Kincho," I say. The dog looks at me and smiles and

169

barks again, then he goes back to pawing Alphonse, who is ruffling his neck feathers and making a big to-do, as my dad would say.

Yvette seems glad to see me. "This is your dog, is it not?" she says.

Alphonse doesn't look up but I know he's listening. So is Kincho, but, then, I don't think he understands English.

"Well, he used to be my dog," I say cautiously.

Yvette puts her hands to her face. "Sacrebleu," she says. "But this is not right. The dog should be with his proper owner." Then, before I can say anything more, she turns to Alphonse and starts talking to him rapid-fire. He ignores her, and just keeps playing with Kincho.

"Alphonse," she says, stamping her foot. "Ecoute!"

"Madame Yvette," I say. "It's okay. Really. I mean, the dog is a lot happier with Monsieur Alphonse than he was with us."

"But no," she says. "What about your family?"

"They don't mind. And I think Kincho—that's what we called him—must have belonged to someone who spoke French before. He never listened to us, never did anything he was supposed to. He's so much better now. And . . . well, to tell you the truth—and if it's okay with you—we're kind of happier without him."

Yvette frowns, but then she watches her uncle playing and smiles. "Well, then, everyone is happy, non?"

I nod. Now Alphonse glances at me and smiles. Kincho smiles, too, but I think it's just a coincidence.

"*Merci bien,*" says Alphonse. He holds out his hand. We shake on it. He winces a little and places his hand over his shoulder, where Annie shot him. "A war wound, eh?" he says, winking at me.

Then he finds a stick and throws it for Kincho. He wanders off, leaving me with Yvette. She doesn't seem in a hurry, so we sit on a bench and I ask her about her uncle and the Vandoos. Partly, I just want to hear her French accent.

"He received a medal for bravery in France," she says, "defending hill . . . *trois-cinq-cinq* . . . three-five-five. *C'est vrai, Alphonse?*"

He doesn't reply. He's too busy playing with his new dog.

"They number the hills in France?"

Yvette laughs. "*Non,*" she says. "I do not think it is so. Maybe they just number the hills in war. Anyway, he got gassed. Mustard gas, and it screwed him up bad."

"Mustard gas?" I'm imagining bombers filled with French's mustard. But it's not like that at all.

"It burns out your lungs and eyes and throat," says Yvette.

"Is that why he looks kind of yellow?"

"*Oui, jaune,*" she says. Then she sighs. "War is a terrible, cruel thing."

That is the end of the panther, but it's not the end of this story. I have no idea where the real Tronido got to, but he fades out of our lives almost right away. We stop talking about him. Even Kathy. One day, when I'm at the fort, I look inside the garbage can and the scrapbook is gone.

... AND AGAIN

The world ends on September 18, which is more than a month before Monsieur Alphonse Lafontaine predicted.

Afterward, everyone tells me that we were warned. "It was in all the papers. It was on the radio and television. Your folks must have said something to you."

If they did I don't remember. Maybe Mum mentioned it at dinner.

"Children, you all know the world is ending on Tuesday, don't you? Anyone want some more cauliflower?"

People tell me that the principal must have warned us over the PA system just after we sang the national anthem.

"There will be no soccer after school today because the world is ending."

I'm pretty sure I would have remembered that.

I don't. Kathy, who is in Miss Cinnamon's class with me, doesn't remember it either. Buster and Sami, who are in Mr. Gallup's class—they don't remember him saying anything.

James, who didn't get sent away to school after all, is also in Mr. Gallup's class. He didn't hear about it.

All our adults failed us.

So there we are, Kathy and I, walking up Lyon, just past First Avenue, when the sirens start. The air-raid sirens. I've never heard them before, not for real. In movies, sure— movies about the Battle of Britain. But not in Ottawa.

Kathy and I look all around, trying to see where the sound is coming from. I tell myself it's a fire engine or an ambulance, but I know it isn't. I know exactly what it is because it's a sound we've been thinking about even if we didn't know we were thinking about it. Except it is more deafening than any of us expected. And even though it sounds so close, we can't see where this horrible noise is coming from.

I don't know who starts to cry first, Kathy or me. Partly, it's the noise. It's so loud it hurts. It's as if they are trying to kill us with the noise so we won't have to die from the bomb or the fallout.

And if it is the bomb . . . if it is the H-bomb . . . then . . . well, it doesn't seem fair. I'm only four cards away from having all eighty-eight CFL football cards. I'm only two stars away from ten in math quizzes, which is when you get a special seal of a race car, if you're a boy, or a ballerina, if you're a girl.

And still the sirens wail.

I'm not sure who takes whose hand. But suddenly Kathy and I are holding hands and walking. Why run? We're walking and crying our eyes out. We turn down Clemow Avenue as if we have a plan in mind and we head to my house. Her house is too far away and her mother is working the day shift now.

We go in and Mum is sitting in the big chair in the living room, knitting. I've never seen her sit down in the daytime.

"Shall I get you some cookies?" she asks. She has to yell because even inside the siren is shrill.

I look at Kathy. She doesn't want any cookies.

"No, thank you!" I yell at my mother. Then we head down to the House of Punch—the one in the basement that Annie made, only Annie is still at school, I guess. That seems a shame. All the work she put into it, all the nights she slept here so as not to be caught unawares.

We crawl in, Kathy Brown and I, and sit there. The siren has followed us downstairs, but it isn't quite so loud. We can hear our hearts down here, and they are beating very fast. That's when I decide to show Kathy a *Punch* magazine. I take one of the volumes out of the wall. The space left is like a little narrow window. I'm not really worried about the radiation because I know now that no book can stop it, anyway. Still, it feels safer to be downstairs under this old table surrounded by thick volumes of *Punch*.

I open the heavy, musty-smelling volume on my lap and Kathy moves in close beside me so that our legs are pressed together, and that feels nice. I turn to a page with a cartoon on it and Kathy looks over my shoulder at the joke, a joke with far too many words in the caption. A joke that neither of us understands.

◎ ◎ ◎

It's just a test. That's all. They're testing the air-raid sirens. I think the air-raid sirens got an A+.

When it's over, when the sound stops, there is a ringing in our ears, and Kathy and I listen through it for other sounds of things blowing up or melting. I'm also listening for the heavy clump of footsteps on the basement stairs, which would mean the mutants have arrived.

When the ringing dies down we close the book and crawl out of the House of Punch to see what's up.

Mum is still sitting in her chair by the fireplace in the living room. She's not knitting anymore, just sitting. And it is so strange to see her doing nothing—not cooking or cleaning or ironing—that I run up and give her a little kiss on the cheek. Then Kathy and I go outside.

It's still there, the outside. But something is different. Everything looks just a little brighter. The tree in front of our house is just turning and when I look at it I can see every single leaf. It's as if I'm looking at a gigantic Paint by Numbers and I can see all those lines I am going to have to stay inside of and it's going to be a huge challenge, but I've got the colors I need, a good sharp-pointed brush, and all the time in the world.

. . . AND AGAIN

The papers are full of the Cuban missile crisis. Kennedy and Khrushchev have never been so angry. It doesn't look good. But what can you do?

So we kind of forget about the end of the world for a bit. You can't think about it all the time or you'd go nuts. You get on with things, as Mum would say.

October comes, and one Saturday when I'm riding through the piles of leaves in Adams Park, who should I see but my beatnik friend. He's carrying a guitar in a case. Unless it's actually a machine gun, but he doesn't look like the machine-gun kind. I tell him about capturing the panther.

"You are one sharp cookie," he says. I ask him about the guitar. He says he's got a gig at Le Hibou. "It's a coffeehouse, man." Then he asks me if I want to hear a song he wrote, and he sits on the bench and plays it. It's called "Dump Orbit" and it's all about Alphonse. I clap when it's over and ask him his name, so that when he becomes famous I'll be able to say I knew him.

Another day at the park Kathy and I go into the woods on the north side. Up at the top of the hill we find a house made out of cardboard boxes filled with smelly blankets, odd bits of clothing, and crusts of food. It must be where Dump Orbit stays on the weekends Yvette and her family are away.

It looks deserted. The nights are getting cold.

◎ ◎ ◎

And then October 23 rolls around. It's another Tuesday. When I look out my window in the morning the leaves that are left on the tree outside are burning-red, and the rest are knee-deep on the lawn. The air is as crisp and clean as the sheets Mum hangs on the line out in the yard. Vancouver never looked like this.

I head over to the park after school. There's an old white van parked against the curb with the back doors open. It's *really* white, not pearl or ivory or any of those colors that are usually 1 through 6 in a Paint by Numbers kit.

As I pull up on my bike, I see two men come up the stairs with Alphonse Lafontaine, who's holding on to a bright blue leash with Kincho at the other end of it. The men aren't dragging Alphonse and he's not dragging Kincho, who walks obediently by his side. It's a miracle.

One of the men has his hand on Alphonse's elbow, but in a nice kind of helping way, and the other man is carrying a ratty-looking suitcase. Yvette is walking along behind them, chatting with the guys, her hands in the pockets of a long green cardigan. She is wearing dark glasses and they reflect the red and gold of the trees.

"*Bonjour*, Rex," she says.

"*Bonjour*, Madame Yvette."

The men are dressed in white that is as white as the van, and it's almost as if they are angels. Except one of them doesn't have very good teeth and the other didn't get too close a shave that morning.

"Are you taking him to the funny farm?" I ask.

They all laugh, even Alphonse.

"No," says one of the not-quite angels. "We're taking our friend here home."

"His new friend is coming, too," says the other, and pats Kincho on the head. "They're going to love this fella at Sunset Acres."

Alphonse pats the dog. "Good old Panthère," he says. Then he looks at me. "You like his name?"

"It's perfect," I say.

Then Yvette explains that Alphonse is going to a retirement home for the winter. In the summer he will come and live with her and her family again.

"He's got lots of buddies there," says the angel with the bad teeth. "Right, Al?"

"*Oui,*" says Alphonse. "*Mes amis d'autrefois. La Guerre.*"

"Did he say something about the war?" I ask. I'm learning.

"*Oui,*" says Yvette. "Friends from the old days. The War."

"The war to end all wars," says Bad Teeth.

"Until the next war to end all wars," says Yvette.

"And the one after that," says Bad Shave.

Alphonse nods at the mention of all these wars. "*C'est ça,*" he says, shrugging. "What are you going to do?"

It is a good question, but nobody tries to answer it. I guess there is no answer. They are on the sidewalk beside the van now and Alphonse looks pretty weary from his hike up the stairs. He stops to catch his breath.

Yvette pats his arm. Then she takes off her dark glasses and kisses her uncle on both cheeks. Everybody says goodbye. The angels help to get Alphonse and Panthère settled in the back of the van. Then they hop in the front and off they go.

And so the world ends for Mr. Alphonse Lafontaine just exactly when he expected it to. Except it's not the end. Just a trip to another place.

I have made a lot of those trips. I know how he must feel. But it's not so bad. You get used to it. The world ends and then it doesn't. One world seems to come crashing to a halt and you invent another.

I look around at the fall-bright trees, then down the

steps to Adams Park where the flower gardens have all been put to bed for the winter. But in my head I can still see the flowers and the grass is still green and there are mothers and babies and summers to come in this brand-new world. I think I'd like to stay in it for a good long time.

Not the End

AFTERWORD

Rex Zero and I have a lot in common. We both moved from Vancouver to Ottawa at about the same age and lived in a big old house on Clemow Avenue with a basement full of *Punch* magazines all collected in volumes. Like Rex, I never got the jokes in them, either. There was a quiver of real arrows in the basement of that old house, but I never found the bow.

Both Rex and I tooled around the streets of the Glebe on green Raleigh three-speeds. We both filled at least one jar of pollywogs, and regularly collected pop-bottle caps at the Clemow Smoke Shop in order to go to the stock-car races at Lansdowne Park. It's a wonder we never ran into each other!

We even both had a dog named Kincho. And yes, he ran away. I hope he found a friend who spoke the same language.

I could go on and on, but the truth is . . . well, the truth is something different from this book. Though there are so many bits and pieces of things that really happened tucked into this story, at some point it got away from me and became a work of fiction. Anybody who knows the lovely little park just north of Powell between Bank and Lyon will recognize that it's not really Adams Park. Adams Park is kind of like all the parks of my youth rolled into one.

Memory is a tricky thing, but I can recall a lot of great

dinner-table scenes with my four sisters and one little brother, with Dad joking and my eldest sister doing a killer impression of the queen and Mum asking if anybody wanted any more of anything and, ultimately, my little sister and I rolling around on the floor laughing so hard we weren't making any sound.

And, like Rex, I remember walking home from school one day and hearing the air-raid sirens and thinking it must be the end of the world. I was alone at the time and I sat right down and cried. I was a little older than Rex by then, but I cried anyway. We didn't have all the facts straight, but kids knew well enough what was going to happen if they dropped the big one. In those days, Rex and I and millions of other people all over the world shared the same nightmare that there was going to be a nuclear war at any moment. That's what the Cold War was all about. A lot of sword rattling on the part of the world's superpowers and a lot of knee shaking on the part of everybody else.

If you're ever in Ottawa, you can actually visit the Diefenbunker, which is now a Cold War museum. Going there, while I was researching this book, brought the memories flooding back.

ACKNOWLEDGMENTS

In January 2005 at the winter residency of the Vermont College Masters of Fine Arts in Writing for Children, where I teach, one of the graduating students, Sarah Sullivan, gave a wonderful lecture about how a childhood of moving from place to place influenced her writing. It seemed to me as if what she was saying was that in her writing she was looking for a place to settle down and feel safe. And that made me think of my own childhood and how much we moved, and how I always felt like an outsider. By the time I drove home from Montpelier that January, I knew I wanted to write about my childhood. I was ready!

Before I left home, I had been 175 pages into writing a completely different novel, but I put it aside and wrote this one instead. I want to thank Sarah for making me open the door into that room where all these memories were waiting.

While I was writing *Rex Zero*, my mother died and my family came from all over to gather here in Perth for the memorial service. It was so good to see them all, especially because I was up to my ears in memories of them. I guess I'd better say right here that the characters in the book are nothing like my real brother and sisters! My real brother and sisters are perfect, just like yours are.

I'd also like to thank Yvette d'Entremont, who I've never even met, but who reads my books sometimes to her classes out in Lower West Pubnico, Nova Scotia. She is the one who was kind enough to help me with the French in this book. Apart from being an enthusiastic teacher, she's also a talented singer-songwriter. You can check out her Web site at www.yvettedentremont.com.

And finally, because it can never be said enough, I want to thank Amanda Lewis, my first reader and very best friend. She spent her childhood in New York and Toronto and never knew what an exciting city Ottawa could be, until now!

GOFISH

TIM WYNNE-JONES

What did you want to be when you grew up?
An architect. From the age of eleven. I went to architecture school, too, for three whole years before they kicked me out. They were afraid that if I designed buildings, people would die!

When did you realize you wanted to be a writer?
I started writing songs for a rock band I joined (just after I got kicked out of architecture school). The songs started getting longer and longer and . . . well, eventually they had chapters.

What's your first childhood memory?
Running away from home with a tea cozy on my head.

What's your most embarrassing childhood memory?
It's too embarrassing to tell.

What's your favorite childhood memory?
Sitting at the captain's table on the R.M.S. *Ascania* crossing the Atlantic from England when we emigrated to Canada. Half the passengers (and all of my family) were throwing up because of high seas, so I got invited to sit with the captain. I was four. I had tomato soup.

As a young person, who did you look up to most?
The Cisco Kid. Or maybe Davy Crockett. Or maybe Zorro, the fox so cunning and free.

What was your worst subject in school?
Math.

What was your best subject in school?
Art.

What was your first job?
As a teen I worked in a grocery store. After university, I worked as a book designer for a publishing house.

How did you celebrate publishing your first book?
My first book won a $50,000 prize, so my wife and I went out and bought a new bed!

Where do you write your books?
In the loft that's up the ladder at the top of my house in the country.

Where do you find inspiration for your writing?
Everywhere. And in music.

Which of your characters is most like you?
Rex, except he's way braver than me. And he has more friends than I had when I was his age.

What was your favorite part of moving?
Favorite part? Moving? I *hated* moving. Oh sure, you get to meet new friends, but what was wrong with the old friends? And what about all those new enemies you get to meet?

What advice do you have for kids who have to move?

You could always try getting all your allowance together and buy the house your parents are leaving and then just stay put. Failing that, you could go knocking door to door and see if there is a neighbor who'd like to have an extra kid move in.

Do you have any siblings? Are they like Rex's siblings?

Well, coincidentally, I have exactly the same number of siblings as Rex. Their names are: Jennifer, Diana, Wendy, Bryony, and Philip. I wouldn't want anyone to think they were anything like Rex's siblings. No way. Couldn't happen . . .

Did you have any pets like Kincho? Do you have pets now?

Curiously, we had a pet exactly like Kincho and his name was . . . wait for it . . . Kincho. Insane dog. Now we have a cat. We usually have cats, plural, but our oldest cat died last Christmas. He was twenty-two, which is about 154 in people years, which isn't bad. Anyway, now we're left with CeeCee, who does seem a little bit lonely.

Have you ever been in a bomb shelter?

I have. There's one in the Cold War Museum in Ottawa, in what used to be called the Diefenbunker. Yep, the very place that Rex's dad helped to build. It's very cool and underground, just as it says in the book. And here's the biggest, coolest part of all: there's a Rex Zero room in the museum! I'm not making this up; there really is. If you're ever in Ottawa, check it out. It's his bedroom with all the kinds of things he'd have had.

When you finish a book, who reads it first?

My wife, Amanda.

Are you a morning person or a night owl?
I'm a morning person. (A mourning dove? I mean, if somebody who likes to stay up late is an owl, why can't I be a bird, too?)

What's your idea of the best meal ever?
I love to cook, and my favorite thing to cook is the Spanish dish paella.

Which do you like better: cats or dogs?
Cats.

What do you value most in your friends?
A sense of humor and the desire to talk about interesting stuff that they feel really passionate about.

Where do you go for peace and quiet?
I live on seventy-six acres of bushland.

What makes you laugh out loud?
When I was a kid I loved the Marx Brothers and Freddy the Pig books. Now I love the play/movie *Noises Off*. And . . . oh, lots of things. I love to laugh! And I have a big laugh. Listen: HAHAHAHAHAHA!

What's your favorite song?
"Les Trios Gymnopédies" by Erik Satie. And "Penny Lane" by the Beatles.

Who is your favorite fictional character?
Ratty in *The Wind in the Willows*.

What are you most afraid of?
WereCheezies.

What time of year do you like best?
Autumn.

What's your favorite TV show?
I mostly don't watch TV, except I love NFL football.

If you were stranded on a desert island, who would you want for company?
My wife, Amanda . . . and, maybe, the complete works of William Shakespeare.

If you could travel in time, where would you go?
Back to last Tuesday.

What's the best advice you have ever received about writing?
Enjoy it! Play at it. Leave the work until later.

What do you want readers to remember about your books?
Where they were sitting when they finished them.

What would you do if you ever stopped writing?
Join another band. But now I'd sing jazz songs.

What do you like best about yourself?
My three children.

What is your worst habit?
Picking my ears!

What do you consider to be your greatest accomplishment?
Seriously? I guess being able to do what I want in life and help

to support a family of kids who are now going off to do what they want.

Where in the world do you feel most at home?
Here, I guess. But I'd also like to live on the southwest coast of England.

What do you wish you could do better?
Play the bass.

What would your readers be most surprised to learn about you?
I read with J. K. Rowling (and Ken Oppel) at the Toronto SkyDome. There were 20,000 people there. It's in *Guinness World Records* as the biggest reading ever. Truly!

A LITTLE BLACK BOOK FILLED WITH NAMES.
A BEAUTIFUL WOMAN WITH A BLACK EYE.
AN EVIL SUBSTITUTE TEACHER.
REX ZERO (AKA DR. LOVE) IS THE ONLY ONE
WHO CAN SOLVE ALL THESE MYSTERIES.

KEEP READING FOR AN EXCERPT FROM

REX ZERO, KING OF NOTHING

BY TIM WYNNE-JONES.

OUR MISTRESS DAY

I t always rains on Our Mistress Day. That's what I'm hoping for tomorrow, freezing November rain as sharp as vaccine needles. The kind of rain my mother would never let me go out in.

"It's called Remembrance Day," says James.

"Except in the States," says Buster. "They call it Veterinarians Day."

"Veterans Day," says Kathy, rolling her eyes.

Buster laughs as if he was fooling. You can never tell with Buster.

"Well, my dad calls it Our Mistress Day," I tell them. "I don't know why. But I hope it rains even worse than this. I hope it pours."

It's Saturday, November 10, 1962, and the four of us are watching the protesters on Parliament Hill in Ottawa. The rain has made their BAN THE BOMB signs bleed. They're waiting for Prime Minister Diefenbaker to show his face. Canada doesn't have any bombs, I don't think—not like the U.S.A. and Russia. Last month they had a fight about Cuba and almost started World War III. I'm not sure Diefenbaker can do much to stop them, but the protesters seem to think he can.

"Where's Dief the Chief!" they shout. "Where's Dief the Chief!"

"Yeah, where *is* Dief the Chief?" says Kathy impatiently.

"Ah, he's not going to show," says Buster.

"He'd better," says Kathy. "I've got a thing or two to tell him." And she will, if she gets the chance. She's very brave. Like her dad, a pilot who got killed in the Korean War.

"Where's Dief the Chief!" shouts Kathy. "Where's Dief the Chief!"

"I think Buster's right," says James. "The prime minister's probably sitting in front of his fireplace listening to the game on the radio."

"Holy moly!"

I totally forgot. The Ottawa Rough Riders are playing the Montreal Alouettes in the Eastern Conference quarterfinals.

I look at James's watch. I have to rub away the beads of rain on the crystal. Two o'clock. Kickoff time.

"Diefenbaker is from Saskatchewan," says James, "so he's probably hoping Ottawa loses."

"Why?" says Kathy.

"Because of the Saskatchewan Roughriders."

"There are two teams called the Rough Riders?" Kathy knows lots of things but football isn't one of them. "Isn't that confusing?" she asks.

"The Saskatchewan Roughriders are out west," says Buster. "In Saskatchewan."

"And they're spelled differently," says James. "The Saskatchewan team is just one word, Roughriders."

"Yeah, but what if both teams made it to the Grey Cup and you were listening to it on the radio, so you couldn't tell who was who," I say.

"The Rough Riders are passing," I say in my best broadcaster's voice. "Oh, no! The Roughriders have intercepted! Look, the Roughriders are trying to block the Rough Riders who are trying to tackle the Roughriders. Hooray, they've scored. The Roughriders have scored!"

Everybody laughs. Then suddenly Kathy is grabbing my arm, jumping up and down, and pointing to the line of protesters.

"In the red tam with the yellow pom-pom. See? See? Isn't that Miss Cinnamon?"

It is. Our sixth grade teacher—the best teacher ever. Except she left, about two weeks ago, because she's expecting a baby.

"I still don't get how she can be *Miss* Cinnamon if she's having a baby," says Buster.

"Because she isn't married," says Kathy. "You don't have to be married to have a baby."

"That's the part I don't get," says Buster.

"Well, Kathy's mom is a nurse, so she'd know," says James.

And Buster and I both agree.

Just then Miss Cinnamon sees us and waves. We all wave back. She's hanging on to the arm of a tall man with a beard. He waves, too.

"I guess their sign says it all," says Kathy.

"BAN THE BOMB! SAVE THE WORLD FOR OUR CHILDREN," reads the sign in the tall man's hands.

"Yeah," says James to Kathy and me. "But who's going to save *you*?" He and Buster are in Mr. Gallup's class. Kathy and I are stuck with the replacement teacher from hell, Miss Garr.

I look at Kathy, still waving. Then she drops her hand and her shoulders sag. Miss Garr is pretty scary, all right. My dad told me a gar is a kind of fish with a long snout and lots of teeth. Some people call them needlefish. Well, that's Miss Garr. She likes to needle people.

I pat Kathy on the shoulder. She shakes me off.

"It's cold," she says. "Let's go."

We're all shivering. Home begins to seem like a really good idea. I leap on my trusty Raleigh three-speed, and we peel out of there so fast the protesters' shouts are soon just a distant murmur.

The rain isn't hard but it's steady, and you have to squint when you get into high gear. Hey, maybe I'll catch pneumonia! Then it won't even matter if the weather is horrible tomorrow. They can't make me go if I'm in the hospital. I swerve to hit a puddle.

It isn't fair. I have three older sisters, as well as a younger sister and brother, but I'm the only one in the family who has to go with Dad to the War Memorial tomorrow for the Our Mistress Day service.

"There'll be real soldiers with guns," says Buster.

"There'll be marching bands with three hundred thousand bagpipers," says James.

"You should feel proud," says Kathy.

"I am proud," I say, but I don't sound it. "It's going to be so boring. I just know it." They all agree. What I really want to say is that I'm scared, scared of letting my father down. But I can't tell them that. And I can't tell them why.

I make it home in time for the second quarter of the game, but Mum won't let me listen to the radio until I change into pajamas. Then I sit in the living room with Dad in front of *our* fireplace with a blanket around me and my feet in a tub of hot water, drinking barley soup from a mug and listening to *our* Rough Riders lose.

"You could have caught your death of cold," Mum says, tucking me in.

"Good," I mutter. "Then I won't have to go to the memorial service." I say this under my breath, but not far enough under my breath.

"What was that?" says Dad. His eyebrows are all

bunched together into one huge, hairy eyebrow, and every hair looks angry.

"Nothing."

He looks toward the ceiling. "Must be those pesky little no-see-ums. I could have sworn I heard a teensy insectlike voice complaining about something."

I look for no-see-ums until I think he's stopped glaring at me. I check. He's looking into the fire. I don't think he's listening to the game. I can hardly hear it myself. All I can think about is tomorrow.

"Our Mistress Day."

"What did you say?"

I didn't realize I had said it out loud. "Our Mistress Day."

"It's *Armistice* Day," says Dad, spelling it out. "Good grief, Rex."

"Armistice? What's that?"

"Truce," says my father. "The end of the war." He puffs away at his pipe. "It comes from the old Swahili word meaning no more lumpy porridge."

I'll never understand how my father can be funny when he's in a foul mood, and he *is* in a foul mood, that's for sure.

"The Americans call it Veterans Day," I tell him.

"Trust the Yanks," says my father. "They didn't even join the bloody war until they'd finished bloody dessert. The Brits and the Canadians had been slogging through the mud since bloody breakfast."

It's a three-bloody sentence, which means he is really riled.

It's halftime in the football game and we're sitting there in the living room, just the two of us, silent now. I don't know what to say. Nothing? That seems like a good idea. Then Mum comes in with more soup for me and another corned beef and Branston pickle sandwich for Dad. There is a furrow in his forehead you could park a Pontiac in.

"Our Mistress Day," he says again. "Did you hear that, Doris?"

Mum is tucking my blanket around me. She looks as if she has her own foul mood she's working on and doesn't want to be interrupted.

"Do you think war is some kind of blooming love affair, Rex?" says Dad.

I've seen the documentaries on TV. I've seen the shrapnel wounds in my father's knee. I know war isn't any fun, which is why we should just get over it, shouldn't we?

"The war ended in 1945, right?" I say. "That's seventeen years ago. Why should we keep remembering all that horrible gunky stuff?" Especially if you have to remember it standing in the pouring rain in scratchy flannel pants, I want to add. But from the expression on Dad's face, I think I'd better shut up. He looks as if he is going to raise his voice, but then he snaps his mouth shut and just fills his pipe instead. His eyes are full of something, though.

A storm. Bigger than the one outside.

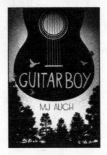